E.L. RHODES

A FLAMING ROSE

A Novel

A FLAMING ROSE

Copyright © 2007 by E.L. RHODES

ISBN 978-1-60530-473-1

Book Cover By: Walter Brinkley

Author Photo By: Glenn Williams

Edited By: Yeng Hsu

This book is dedicated to the woman who has held my heart since my first breath, Vera. Mom, thanks for all the sacrifices that you made through the hard times. You helped make those hard times always seem like good times. I love you, and keep up the good fight.

Acknowledgments

I would like to first thank my Creator, who despite all of my imperfections, calls me His own.

I would like to thank everyone who supported and assisted with this work: Marty Swann, Michele "Mt" Tyner, Nicole Rhodes, Jan Brinkley, Ms. Garland and The Beauregard Book Club. Thank you all for taking time from your busy schedules to read this manuscript and provide the constructive criticism and feedback that you did.

To my kids, Twan, Stephanie "Fuzzy", and Genee' "Yokie", you are my life. Jasmine, I miss you. I love you all. I know you all think that I'm crazy sometimes but it's just love...sike, I'm really crazy (smile).

To my sisters, Shirley, Pearl, Wanda, and Kathy, thank you for always supporting me, and all the laughter. I love you all.

To my friend and brother, Walt, thanks for all that you do. You stand by me even when you know I've lost my mind. You are one of the most talented people I know and yet the humblest. I haven't got the words.

To Glenn, you laugh, you snap the pictures, you laugh, you snap the pictures. Thanks for always having my back even though you're from Buffalo.

To all my old neighborhood friends; Nate, Bel, Bob J, Joe Sponge, and all the HiFChap folks, thanks for the memories and material. Your story should be told, maybe later.

To Cheryl "Lula" Price, you have been my inspiration since the beginning. You are always in my heart with each line that I write. I miss you.

To a very special person, a very special thank you. Yeng Hsu, thank you for all the hard work and dedication that you have put into this. You've worked harder on this than I have. Thank you, thank you, thank you. You are truly the air that I breathe. Without you, this would not have happened. I love you.

If I've left anyone out, it was not intentional. You all know that the mind is the first thing to go, but thank you.

CHAPTER 1   THE MAN

"Damn! Damn! Damn, I'm fine. Boy, you should be posin' for Play Girl." Just stepping out of the shower, standing in front of the mirror flexing his hidden muscles and talking to himself, was the hunk of man that all women desired. Okay, maybe not all women, but most. Well, not most, but some. Ah what the hell, maybe just one. You see, in reality, he was big boned, overweight, and extremely obnoxious. He had a gap in his front teeth wide enough to kick a field goal through, short nasty dread locks, and had rolls on the back of his neck that had the appearance of about three unwrapped Vienna Sausages. And regardless of what the temperature was inside or out, he always had at least four beads of sweat on the tip of his nose. At 5' 7" tall and 236 pounds of moist flab, Melvin Dossier was the man; well at least in his mind.

In the mailroom where he was the shift supervisor, Melvin made sure everybody knew that he was in charge. Always reminding his subordinates of extended breaks, lunch, or minor screw-ups, he prided himself on being a tyrant. Oh yeah, he was truly full of himself, the man.

Although he thought he was king of the mailroom, he was known as "The Campbell's Soup Boy" by everyone else. His armpit odor was his trademark. Most of the people who worked there complained about his split pea and onion smell, while others only tolerated it and talked about him behind his back.

He would flirt with every woman in the building, but there was only one that truly had his eye. He adored her. She was Wendy Parker, the administrative assistant on the seventh floor for one of the company's VPs. Wendy was tall, lean, and had the longest, sexiest, bowed legs that she had no problem displaying from underneath the glass table top of her desk. She was a quiet woman by appearance, but had attitude. She was a very confident woman who knew how to handle customers and Melvin. Her dark skin and short hair gave her a kind of boyish look that was attractive to both genders. After his coffee and honey bun, Melvin always made the mail run on the seventh floor just to see those legs and to get in some flirt time. He'd always start by leaning over her desk then blurting out one of his usual suave and sophisticated complimentary lines.

"Damn baby, I'd like to climb up those long ass legs," or "Girl, you know what they say, once you go fat, you'll never go back! Come on let me throw a picnic in that back yard of yours."

Oh yeah, he was smooth, not. Wendy would always listen to his morning greeting, get the mail and then end their brief visit with a sophisticated line of her own.

"Go to hell Melvin, and on your way, stop and hose down those musty arm pits, with your Campbell's soup smellin' ass."

That would be music to Melvin's ears, because in his mind that was just her way of flirting back. As for Wendy, she hated his guts.

Upon his return to the mailroom, he'd always lie about all the women that wanted him and how Wendy couldn't resist him.

"Oh yeah, I can hit that anytime I want!" he'd brag, but everybody in the mailroom knew that he was living in "Fiction City". They knew that he was further from reality than anyone in the building. He couldn't buy a date. The truth of it is, I believe he only approached women because he knew they'd turn him down. Others thought this as well.

One day, as a test, one of the women from the mailroom started flirting back with Melvin. She told him that she would love to go out with him sometime. Everyone could see that this made him a bit nervous, especially since she wasn't one of the dusty swamp rat hussies that he would usually approach.

"So how about it Mel?" she advanced.

Melvin's defense mechanism immediately kicked in.

"Look here girl, uh, you don't want to do that. This here is Melly Mel the Master! I'll rock that world of yours. Turn your ass out! Then you'd do nothin' more than get on my nerves worryin' the hell out of me. Callin' ten times a day just to hear my voice, I don't have time for that. As a matter of fact, do you know why most women use these two fingers to get off?"

Melvin held up his index and middle fingers pressed tightly together up in the air. The woman glared at his two chubby fingers and then back at the other spectators in the office. They too had no clue as to what the answer to Melvin's question was. She looked back over to Melvin and responded.

"Well no, I can't say that I do."

Melvin lowered his fingers down to his mouth. He stuck out his thick wide bumpy tongue and licked them right up the center.

He looked her right in the eye then spoke calmly, "Because, they're mine."

The entire break room erupted in laughter. Melvin had saved himself and his fictional reputation.

After work, Melvin would usually head over to his favorite watering hole, The Sapphire. He would sit and drink with others of the same sort, and talk sports for hours before heading to his cracker box apartment over in the South East section of D.C. His buddy Dave was also one of his scheduled stops on his way home. These two had been friends since GI Joes and pop rocks. They came up through the times together. They were boys back when Chuck Taylors, and red, black, and green sweat socks were the thing. When styling elephant leg bell bottom jeans, bell sleeve shirts with a medallion, and stack heeled shoes labeled you as being hip. They were hanging out when the two-toned, padded shoulder shirts, wide legged "MC Hammer" pants, and run over heeled shoes for some strange reason qualified you as being "down by law". Anyway, yeah, they were a couple of clowns that have been together for quite sometime. Melvin would try to stop in on Dave as much as he could.

Dave's place was like the neighborhood recreation center. Dave had all the important necessities required by the average adult male. He had PlayStation, PlayStation 2, XBOX, the Internet, air hockey, ping pong, a pool table, HD TV with all the cable stations, and satellite television; he even had a damn ATARI. He had beer, chips, porn, and above all, he had weed.

Now weed was one of Melvin's favorite past times. Weed was his best friend that is, next to Dave. In fact, if he had a child, his child would be named "Weed Dossier". Although he had a great love for his child, he never paid support. Meaning, he did love his son "Weed", but always got a free handout from Dave. He'd stop by Dave's and smoke until he couldn't see past his hands and then would leave with a ten dollar bag. Well, a ten dollar bag for most that is. Dave would never charge Melvin and Melvin knew this.

Now Dave was no mailroom clerk, but he wasn't an attorney or a doctor, either. Can you say "drug dealer"? Yep, Dave was a dealer, but let's give him some credit because Dave would only sell weed. No crack, no coke, no crystal meth, and no heroin; just weed, and he wouldn't sell to kids, either. Let's just say he was a dealer with a heart, if there is such a thing.

Seven years ago, Melvin and Dave worked together. They were both runners for Lucas, the neighborhood drug dealer. They used to go everywhere with Lucas until one day Melvin found himself looking down the barrel of a .38 caliber revolver. He was scared shitless. He wasn't alone, either. Both Lucas and Dave were right beside him. It was a drug deal that had gone bad, real bad. Melvin did everything that he could not to look like a little punk by fainting, whereas Lucas was just the opposite. He never stopped cursing the guys and making threats. Dave was just as calm as Lucas, which was just as scary to Melvin. He was on the verge of falling to his knees and crying and begging for his life when Lucas started walking toward the gunman and told him that if he shot him he'd better kill him.

"What kind of monkey bullshit is that?" Melvin thought. He knew right then and there that being a drug dealer was not his intended occupation. He knew a life like this couldn't last very long.

As the argument became even more heated his life had started to pass before his eyes, followed by his bowels. Without hesitation, Melvin turned and ran as fast as he could. He heard gunfire and cursing in the distance and looked back just once.

Melvin woke up the next morning with his head and his right butt cheek wrapped in bandages. He again realized that being a drug dealer was not the life for him. Seems that when he turned to look back, he had gotten shot right in the backside and ran head first into a telephone pole. Go figure. Lucas was killed that night, but Dave had managed to get away. Later that week, the gunman and his accomplice were both found dead in Anacostia Park. Some say it was Dave's doing, but the case was never solved.

Over the next seven years, Dave had become the new Lucas of the neighborhood. He had become the king; the Godfather. Melvin and Dave remained best of friends, but they always knew where to draw the line. Melvin would stop by occasionally and play video games, listen to music, and would always get high with Dave. They'd talk for awhile about the old days. This would occur usually after already having had a few at The Sapphire. He'd stop by Dave's to take it just a little higher, then he'd go home to think about Wendy and jack himself off to sleep.

CHAPTER 2   THE LETTER

This morning was no different than any other. Melvin went through his usual ritual. He got up, ate a bowl of oatmeal, and took his morning constitutional, showered and then rummaged through the dirty clothesbasket for something to wear.

He'd check his mailbox about every four days or so on the way out to work, because he was usually too stoned or drunk to remember to check it when he got home most days. He always took his mail to work and threw all of the unwanted or unpayables in the dumpster by the loading dock.

This particular morning, Melvin found a strange looking envelope in his mailbox. It had a fancy logo in the upper left hand corner. He stood in the hallway of his building staring at the envelope. It didn't even have a stamp on it. This was beyond his normal Sports Illustrated or his copy of the Victoria Secrets catalog. It wasn't even the every other month eviction notice either. No, this was something different, something important.

He slipped the letter into the inside pocket of his Members Only jacket and climbed into his 1979 Ford Escort and headed for work.

Melvin arrived at work at 7:45 a.m., his usual time. He went down and got his coffee then set up shop in front of the time clock like he did every morning so that he could monitor his folks clocking in down to the second. By 9:00 a.m. he was headed up to the seventh floor to put in his daily bid. After his "go to hell" from Wendy, Melvin was headed back downstairs when he heard someone call him from the office across from the elevator.

"Young man, young man, may I speak with you for a moment?"

Melvin wasn't quite sure what to do. "Did I give her the wrong mail?" he thought, "or is somethin' missin' from her office and she wants to blame me like they did Terrence?"

Melvin turned slowly and glanced into the office. There he saw a scrawny older woman sitting behind a desk with her glasses pulled down to the tip of her nose. She had silver grayish hair and wore a white blouse that looked too big for her. She also had huge protruding breasts that strained from behind the fabric.

"You're going about it the wrong way," she said, while appearing to be swallowed up by her blouse.

"What's that?" Melvin asked.

"The young lady, she's never going to go out with you if you keep approaching her like that."

Curious, Melvin walked into the woman's office and they began to talk. They talked about women, style, and how women responded to men. Melvin thought that he would just appease the older woman at first, but he soon became engrossed in their conversation. The woman schooled him in every aspect of womanizing. Mel was so impressed with the vast amount of information she had given him that he offered to take her to lunch to show his gratitude.

"I know a nice chicken and rib buffet joint right over the bridge," Melvin stated all the while smiling like he had just discovered his first erection.

The little woman looked at Melvin with the sweetest smile, as if she was about to blush from the mere thought of him asking her out.

"Have you not heard a word that I've said? Really! Do I look like a woman who would go to a rib buffet and slap on one of those silly looking rib bibs to sit down and gorge on ribs and chicken until I felt as if I was going to burst?"

Melvin's smile slowly faded and the woman now had a look of anger on her face.

"Thank you, but I think I'll pass. And if you really understand what I've been trying to tell you, then YOU wouldn't be thinking about ribs. YOU would be thinking about jogging your fat ass to the nearest salad bar to have a fat free salad without dressing and a small diet water only. Do you see what I'm talking about? You've got no class young man. So why would that young lady want to go out with somebody like you? You're overweight, dressed like you're headed to a dog fight, and no offense, but you smell like chicken and onions. I'm just tired of hearing you morning after morning getting shot down. It's really pathetic, that's what it is. You seem like a nice guy, but what is it that you young people say?... oh yes, you've got no game young man. No game at all."

After being torn into by the lady, Melvin backed out of the doorway with his tail between his legs. His ego had been set ablaze and extinguished with urine. He looked up at the woman and nodded his head.

"Game huh? I gotcha, and maybe you're right. She is kind of outta my league. Thanks. I'll work on it, my game that is. Next time you see me I won't be playin' tag, I'll be playin' chess."

"That's the spirit young man."

Melvin smiled and thanked the woman again then left her office.

After making his way back down to the mailroom, in all the confusion and lecturing, he had forgotten all about the envelope that he had in his jacket. He grabbed a soda and a biscuit from his lunch bag, took out the envelope and sat down at his desk. "Kohl, Swann, and Goldberg, Attorneys at Law" was stamped on the upper left hand corner. Mel opened the envelope and pulled out a letter and a business card. He stuffed the business card in his pants pocket and started reading the neatly typed letter. The letter requested his presence at their law office. Seeing how he had his dealings with the law, he thought what any other man in his position would think.

"What in the hell did I do?"

He peered out of the window and saw Wendy getting into her Honda Civic and drive away. He thought about what the old woman had said, looked down at his biscuit, and pinched one of the love handles that rested on the side of his gut and walked over to the trashcan and chucked the biscuit in.

"There's no way in hell that I'm goin' to some lawyer's office. This can't be nothin' but trouble."

Melvin ripped up the letter and dropped the torn pieces into the trashcan on top of his unbitten biscuit.

He thought for a second and then yelled, "Damn! What in the hell am I doin'?"

He reached back into the trashcan and swept the small pieces of ripped paper to the side and picked up the biscuit. He looked around for a second for witnesses, brushed it off, kissed it and then held it up to the sky. After the ten-second rule had passed, he tore into the cold biscuit.

After a not so long day at work, Mel decided to head on over to Dave's. He figured he'd chat with him about his day, his newly learned knowledge of women, and his letter. He knocked on the door. After several minutes, Dave opened the door and returned promptly to the couch. Melvin stepped in and headed straight for the fridge. He reached down on the bottom shelf and retrieved a tall bottle of Miller's Genuine Draft.

"What's shakin' Dave?"

"This big Johnson of mine; twice after I'm done pissin'; and then I'm fine! What the fuck you think's shakin'?"

Mel sat down and popped open the cold brew.

"Damn man, you ever thought about writin' for Hallmark? I mean you're just so sensitive and poetic. This big Johnson of mine... then I'm fine! Wow! That's real talent there."

Dave just sat there mumbling to himself with his face frowned up.

"Hard day for da man today?" he mumbled.

"Sheeeeeit, the MAN don't run me dog!" Melvin boasted.

Dave turned, looked at Melvin, blew out the smoke that he had been holding for a few seconds then leaned into Melvin and whispered, "Whatever!"

They both started laughing and Dave passed Mel the joint. They played Madden '07 and talked about back in the day.

Then right out of the blue, Melvin spewed out, "Man, some punk ass lawyers sent me a letter today talkin' bout my presence was needed or some shit like that."

Melvin blew out some smoke then continued, "I mean, what? They think I'm stupid or somethin'? Aint no way I'm goin' down there so they can fine me, or tax me, or tell me bout some ho who's been lookin' for her baby's daddy, I aint tryin' to go through that man. Havin' me feelin' like I'm on the Maury show: In the case of four year old Shanneikwa, Melvin YOU ARE THE FATHER! Oh hell no, not this boy!"

Melvin, now feeling the effects from the twisted cigarette, was now staring down at his crotch and gritting his teeth. Dave held out his hand for the joint, but Mel just kept on smoking and staring. Dave leaned back on the plaid couch and folded his arms across his chest. He leaned over towards Mel with a serious look.

"You're stupid if you don't know that a letter from a law firm automatically means money. Money you owe, or money that's owed to you, and since you aint got shit that you owe for, somebody must have some money for you, fool. Oh yeah, and by the way, you have to actually fuck somebody first, to be called her baby's daddy. So bein' that you aint never had no pussy, I don't think you'll have to worry about that one. Nope, you don't need to be worryin' that the Maury Show will be callin' your ass. It aint gonna happen. Now Jerry Springer on the other hand, that's a strong possibility. You'll be on that show where the best friend has whupped yo ass for not passin' the joint!"

Melvin leaned forward and turned to Dave with squinting eyes, now speaking loudly as if his consumption of weed had somehow turned him deaf.

"Sheeeeeeit, what you talkin' 'bout boy? For all you know, I just might be your daddy. Your mother was askin' me to go down and have another blood test just the other day 'cause you know your brother's mine. You know, you do have my eyes."

Dave looked at Melvin with a strange crooked smile. He held out his hand and whispered, "Is Jerry Springer gonna have to fly us out there?"

Melvin took another long draw from the twisted cigarette then passed it over to Dave. He sat quietly for a few minutes with his eyes half closed. Finally, he was able to get out his question that had him concentrating so hard. He leaned toward Dave and tried to speak. He stuttered for a second before he was able to push out his powerful question, "Word?"

Dave inhaled deeply from the marijuana stick. He turned to Mel, blew out his smoke and whispered, "Word man!"

Both men sat on the couch for over an hour, high, blank faced and speechless.

The next morning was unlike any other. Mel didn't eat his oatmeal, didn't have his morning constitution, and didn't even pull an already worn shirt from his dirty laundry. Instead, Mel sat on the side of his bed thinking about what to do. Sitting there with blood shot eyes, a slight headache, and feeling light headed from his lack of sleep, he slowly reached over to his make shift nightstand: a milk crate which was covered with a piece of plywood and had a pillow case draped over the top. He retrieved the small business card that had been inside the folded letter. He picked up his cell phone off the nightstand and dialed the number of the law office.

After the second ring Mel heard a soft but raspy voice gently say, "Kohl, Swann, and Goldberg, Attorneys at Law, how may I assist you?"

Mel paused for a second and then without thinking spouted out, "Uh, uh yeah, y'all sent me a letter about seein' me."

The voice paused for a second, and then asked, "Your name sir?"

There was no answer.

After a long silence and two long deep breaths he answered, "Melvin... Melvin Dossier."

The soft raspy voice asked him to hold the line while she retrieved the information. Melvin sat on the side of his bed biting down on his already mauled fingernails as he rocked back and forth listening to the sound of the clicking of the computer keyboard through the receiver.

"Yes Mr. Dossier, we sent you a letter a few days ago. We need you to come in to discuss a matter regarding your uncle Cleveland."

Melvin sat quietly thinking to himself, "I haven't seen that jackass in years. What does he want from me? He's always hated me. This can't be good."

Melvin tried to get more information from the lady but was unsuccessful. He finally agreed to come down to the office the following day. Melvin jumped up, slammed his cell phone back on his less than sturdy nightstand, and jumped in the shower.

After arriving at work, Melvin was as quiet as a young lady who had just passed gas in church. He spoke to not a single soul throughout the whole day. He didn't monitor anyone's time, didn't check the sort bins for errors, and he didn't even make his seventh floor run. He walked around all day like he was in a trance. By the end of the day, he decided to stop by The Sapphire.

Sitting on his usual bar stool sipping on a rum and coke, he started to think back, back to when he and his uncle "Cleve" were around each other. He recalled that Uncle Cleve always acted as if he never really liked him much and how he always used the word "shit" in just about every statement that came out of his mouth. He remembered how Uncle Cleve loved his mother so much, but how he changed so much after moving away.

He was a big man; a man who didn't take any foolishness from anybody.

It was said that Uncle Cleve once beat a man's head wide open with a pipe just for scratching his testicles while riding in his car. Some say that he busted the guy's head all the way back to the white meat, too. Some said he was just flat out crazy and some say he was just troubled.

Once, when Melvin was a young teen, Uncle Cleve told him that a friend of his had a summer job for him down at "Sam's Carwash". Melvin was so excited. Uncle Cleve gave Melvin an envelope and told him to take it and give it to the manager and tell him that he was there for the special services job. He told Melvin that the job paid ten dollars an hour.

Back in those days, ten bucks an hour was better than great pay, especially for a young teen. Hell, minimum wage was only a dollar and ten cents per hour.

Melvin caught the bus to the carwash and did what he was instructed. He gave the envelope to the manager, which the manager in turn gave Melvin a folded slip of paper. Melvin then asked the manager about the special services job.

The manager was a close friend of Uncle Cleve's named West Wilkins. He was a very heavy man with fat cheeks, bad acne and perspired like Jessie Jackson at a Klan rally. West looked at Melvin and asked him did he know what they did in special services?

Melvin shrugged his shoulders and said, "It pays ten bucks an hour, right? For that kind of money, who cares? I'm the man for the job."

With this, Big West placed his fat fingers over his even fatter beer belly and laughed loudly.

"Maybe you are kid, maybe you are just the guy we need for this particular job."

West, now laughing hysterically began to wave some of the other employees over to where he and young Melvin stood.

"Guys, this young man is here for special services job. Who wants to train him?"

All of the men stood around laughing and pointing at Melvin. Melvin realized that he was now the brunt of some awful joke, stood there looking ever so embarrassed. He finally asked the question that he knew he really didn't want the answer to.

"So Mr. West, what is the ten dollar an hour job?"

West continued laughing until he was able to calm himself. He stood there bent over with his hands planted firmly on both of his knees to hold himself up. After catching his breath, he answered poor little Melvin.

"Son, there's a long standing joke down here at the car wash. We always tell the new guys on the job that they can transfer to the special services area of the car wash and they'll make ten, sometimes even fifty dollars an hour. When they ask what they'll have to do in special services, we tell them. Special Services is where farts are individually sucked out of the car seats. We ask them to sign a black lung waiver before starting. We also tell them that there is a two week training class to help them prepare their lips."

West started up again and the other guys joined in; the laughter sounded like thunder again.

Melvin thought back on that day and started to laugh himself. It turns out that Uncle Cleve merely owed Big West some money and West returned his "paid in full" IOU. Still Melvin and

Uncle Cleve never had a good relationship, so what could this be about?

Mel kept mumbling. Just as he was about to down the rest of his rum and coke, Mel sat the glass back on the bar and thought to himself, "I'd better have my head together for tomorrow, gotta be ready for 'em."

Mel laid a five dollar bill on the bar next to his almost finished rum and coke and walked toward the stained glass door.

"Catch you guy's lata!" Mel yelled, and slowly stepped outside.

Standing outside of his building taking care of some business, Dave spotted Melvin in his car. He slid his right hand in his pocket and motioned Melvin over to a parking spot with the other.

Mel pulled into the spot and Dave climbed inside the car.

"Wassup my brotha? Did you get a chance to handle yo biz?"

Mel leaned forward and pushed in the cigarette lighter after noticing Dave sliding a Newport out of its pack.

"I go see 'em in the mornin'. They still didn't tell me what it's about, but what the hell, I'll find out then." Dave lit his cigarette, took a drag and opened his door.

"You comin' up?"

"Nah, think I'll just head on home and try to get some sleep. Guess I better try to have my head together for tomorrow. I'll give you a call when I leave that joint. That is, unless I'm escorted somewhere else. Not knowin' what this is all about has me nervous as hell. You know if the man comes up in there actin' foul tryin' to put a brotha in some cuffs, they'll have a fight on their hands."

Dave looked over at Melvin and shook his head.

"Man, if the law comes to snatch up your punk ass, you'd be cryin' like a bitch!"

Dave stepped out of the car, stuck his hand in the window to give Mel some dap. Then he looked down and said, "You know you're missin' two hub caps man?"

Mel leaned back and shook his head and yelled, "Damn! Four caps man! That's all four! Those sons-a-bitches, you can't have shit!"

Pissed off, Mel pulled out of the space and went straight home.

CHAPTER 3   THE APPOINTMENT

In the morning, Mel rummaged through his closet trying to put an ensemble together for his big meeting. So far, he had a pair of fake leather shoes that used to be his dad's, and a pair of green slacks, with just a hint of polyester that he's had since the early '80's which were worn thin on the inner thigh area from his thighs rubbing together. He also found a too small white shirt that he wore with the uniform given to him when he was employed as a security guard at the S&R grocery store some years back. It still had the holes over the upper left pocket that was left from his nametag and was missing three buttons in the front. Then there was the black jacket; the black jacket with the fake belt in the back and two side vents. That was also too small as well. It damned near looked like a butler's jacket, too. The collar had those "polyester knots" on the back that portray what a dead "poly" would look like.

"Where's my damn tie? I know it's here somewhere."

Melvin kept digging in his closet then he pulled out a shoebox from the top shelf. There, way back in the corner of the shelf, lay a balled up orange and blue clip on necktie with kangaroos on it. Melvin threw on his outfit. The pants were so tight, he could hardly move.

"Damn, looks like I might have picked up a couple of pounds since back in the day. These slacks used to be it!"

Melvin pulled and tugged on the trousers until he was able to provide some slight relief for his testicles. He had decided to endure the sharp wedge of slack that was creased into the opening of his buttocks. As he walked, the slight bell bottom of his pants waved just above his ankles and his gut hid the large "V" shaped opening that had formed because of a shortage of material around the waistband. You do the math, fifty goes into thirty four how many times? That's correct, none! He had managed to cram all fifty inches of his waist, butt, and thighs into a size thirty four slack. I guess polyester really does stretch!

After wrestling with the rest of his ensemble, Melvin grabbed his keys and headed out the door. Outside, he sees a figure leaning comfortably against the passenger door of his car. The figure was lean, sleek, yet unaware.

"What the fu…? Man what are you doin' here?"

"You know I couldn't let you face the gators alone."

"Damn, nice suit! Look at you, cleaner than new money! Can't hit you in the ass wit a red apple, huh? I used to have a suit just like that. Looks like my size, too."

"I used to have a suit just like the one you have on, too. I gave it to my cousin; he needed somethin' to put down in his dog's house for him to lie on."

Melvin popped Dave the finger and continued to compliment him.

Dave was wearing a gray Ralph Lauren suit and tie looking like a million bucks.

"C'mon man, we gotta hurry up before we be late," Mel yelled across the top of the car. Dave climbed into the passenger side of the Escort and looked at Mel with a puzzled expression on his face.

"What?" Mel asked.

"Do you realize that you have kangaroos on your tie? Kanga fuckin' roos man, do you realize that shit?"

Mel turned his head and mumbled a few obscenities. Dave inhaled deeply, then placed his index finger underneath his nose and looked back over to Melvin.

"Yo man, you smell soup? Damn, that shit's makin' me hungry."

Melvin threw up his middle finger, turned and sniffed his right armpit. He started the car. Dave reached over and turned the ignition off.

"Change the tie man. I can't be seen with you and Klumpy the Kangaroo. I have an image to uphold in the community."

Melvin once again threw up his middle finger and started the car. And as before, Dave reached over and shut the car off and leaned against the passenger door.

"We are not goin' downtown with Klumpy, and what's with the fur neck collared Soul Train jacket? Your neck's not hot? Look man, it'll only take a couple of minutes to shoot by my house and hook you up. You can't walk in there with those nut crushin' slacks on man. You won't even have any circulation in your legs by the time we get downtown. Do yourself a favor Mel, let me hook you up."

Melvin looked over at Dave in anger and then down at his Eleganza hand picked 1970's to 1980's crossover disco/butler ensemble.

Dave placed his hand on Melvin's shoulder, "Please man, do it for me. I mean, after all that is a security guard shirt you have on. A butler's jacket and a security guard shirt? C'mon man, you look like you should have a flashlight in one hand and a jar of Grey Poupon in the other. And what you tryin' to do? You tryin' to go to Kansas? Man, 'cause with those glass slippers you're wearin', I'm sure you could click your damn heels three times and go anywhere you want. Where in the hell is Toto, huh?"

Melvin finally gave in to Dave. He knew deep inside that he somehow portrayed the image of a Ringling Brothers clown reject. He could even see the reflection of his car keys off the plastic covering of his shoes. He turned, looked at Dave, nodded and they headed for Dave's.

They arrived at Dave's in record time. Although just around the corner, Melvin seemed to be moving at light speed.

As they approached the entrance to Dave's building, they were greeted by some of the neighborhood fellows who normally sat on the steps all day.

"Nice life vest Mel, you guys goin' fishin'?" one of the guys complimented.

"Blow me!" Melvin grunted as he stormed past.

The guys rushed inside Dave's apartment. Dave retrieved a shirt and a jacket for Melvin. Although they were a little tight, he looked much better than before.

"I'm keepin' the tie man and the pants too."

"Yeah whatever! Look here man, think about it. You're actually gonna walk in there in a pair of ball crushin' slacks with two worn out friction holes between the thighs? What if you take that one extra step that tears through the rest of that fabric? Are you really goin' to be comfortable sittin' in front of the attorneys with one of your balls hangin' through a friction hole? I mean, if you're comfortable with that then fine. But I gotta tell you, I on the other hand, really don't feel a real need to be viewin' your nut sack durin' a meetin'. I don't know how they'll feel about it."

"Ok, Ok! I get it. Damn man, do you know how difficult it was for me to squeeze my ass into these pants?"

"You need somethin' to scrape 'em off with?"

"Man, just give me the damn pants."

Dave then passed Melvin a pair of Khaki pants. They were a little tight too, but better than the cotton, plastic, and rayon blend that he had painted on before.

"Ok, that's better, don't you think?" Dave asked. "Aren't those better than those vented nut slacks? I know they don't let your crotch breathe as much, but they're better right?"

Melvin nodded in agreement and out the door they went. They headed back down the steps, rushed into the car and sped off into the traffic.

Downtown was like it always was, crowded. Crowded with people and cars, but for some reason Melvin loved the noise.

"Eighty One Hundred Penn Ave" stuck out prominently above the six glass paneled doors of the building. The address was made of dull copper and sculpted into block letters.

The building itself was very impressive looking. Newly re-novated and towering fourteen stories high, this modern day castle had the look of nothing but money.

Mel and Dave stepped into the huge lobby. They slowly headed toward the solid cherry half moon shaped security desk. From a distance they could see the top of the security guard's head barely peeping out from just above the raised counter top.

The security guard looked up over the rim of her glasses and asked, "And how may I help you gentlemen?"

"We're headin' up to the 14th floor, to Kohl, Swann, and Goldberg's."

The security guard stood up and slid a large signature filled binder in front of Dave. She turned the book around and started scribbling down the left hand side of the page, then spun the book back toward Dave.

"I'm gonna need you both to sign in."

Dave took the pen from the short heavyset woman, scrib-bled for a second and pushed the book over to Melvin. After Melvin whipped out his John Hancock, he placed the book gently in front of the guard. She directed them to the elevators.

She pointed to Dave and said, "Hey, nice suit!" She then turned her eyes over in Melvin's direction as they headed towards the elevator. Melvin looked back. She looked over the rim her eye glasses and with a slight chuckle yelled over to Melvin.

"Your suit is tight, too."

Melvin stopped and looked down at his outfit.

"Why you gotta go there, huh? Why can't a man who's just doing the best that he can get a break? See, its sistas like you who bring us positive brothas down. Always got somethin' to say!

Always gotta let us know how much better you're doin' than us. Woman, please! So what? So I aint bringin' down, six figures. So I'm not... "

Before Melvin could finish, the security guard interrupted him.

"Sir, Sir! I was just remarking that your suit looked nice. You know 'tight' as in real cool or nice. I think you look real handsome. I mean, really handsome. I would never bring a strong man like you down. Look, you have a nice day and if you get a chance, stop down and see me before you leave."

Melvin stood there with his mouth open; feeling a bit embarrassed and yet flattered at the same time. He managed to collect himself and headed for the elevator where Dave was now waiting with a huge smile on his face.

"See what happens when you wear my shit? Chicks just come at you from out the wood work. Even the meanest security guard is mesmerized by the style. Watch out man. That might just be too much power for you to handle!"

The men stepped into the elevator and pushed "14" on the elevator panel. The doors closed.

"See, I told you I should have stuck with my jacket. Wasn't nothin' wrong with that jacket! Besides, this shirt is too tight on my gut."

"Did you write down your real name?" Dave whispered.

"What's that got to do with me not bein' able to breathe man?"

"Did you or didn't you?"

"Yeah man. Why, didn't you?"

Dave leaned over to Melvin and whispered, "Fuck no. I don't know that ho, and if some shit breaks off up in here and I have to step in one of these lawyer's ass on your behalf, I don't want them to know who in the hell I am. Hell, they piss me off, I'm liable to whip my shit out and piss all over their pretty little office. Sheeeit, you know me cuz."

Mel looked at the row of lights above the elevator door, "7… 8…"

He looked over at Dave who was busy brushing off the sleeve of his expensive suit coat still mumbling to himself.

Mel said in a very calm voice, "Maybe you should just wait downstairs bro."

Dave refused to go back to the lobby only to be watched by Ms. "Fake Ass Five-O" as Dave so affectionately referred to her and all security police.

The two stepped off the elevator. They proceeded down the hall through the huge mahogany double doors which carried the same names that appeared on the business card that Melvin had received from the firm, "Kohl, Swann, and Goldberg". Dave reached over and opened the right side of the doors and Melvin stepped in followed by his partner. They approached the reception desk of a somewhat petite and shy looking young lady.

"May I help you gentlemen?" the young lady asked. Melvin recognized the soft, raspy voice.

"Uh yeah, yeah we're lookin' for the lawyer who sent me a letter," Melvin muttered. "I'm Melvin Dossier. That's D-O-S-S-I-E-R."

"Oh yes Mr. Dossier, I believe we spoke yesterday," she said.

"Mr. Kohl is expecting you. Please have a seat and I'll let him know you're here."

Melvin and Dave headed for the big plush rust colored leather seats near the entrance of three office doors. Dave dropped into one of the chairs and crossed one leg over the other. Melvin read the names on the doors then returned to the chairs and sat down beside Dave. He sat there scanning the room and marveled at all the expensive looking paintings that were hung throughout the waiting area.

"Damn, this is nice," Melvin whispered, but not low enough. The receptionist looked over and nodded her head as she smiled at Melvin.

"Even the carpet looks expensive," Melvin continued.

Dave leaned over and ran his hand across the carpet fabric then turned his head upward toward Melvin. "Well I guess that ho must work in the minimum wage section 'cause the carpet starts after her desk."

As Dave giggled, the young lady turned and glared at Dave as she cleared her throat then quickly turned up her nose at both men.

"Oh hell no! Is that attitude I detect? Aint my fault she's on the floor tile. She must have refused to blow the boss! And did that bitch just finish smokin' a pack of Marlboro's or what? That ho sounds like James Earl Jones on crack!" Dave mumbled with a shit-eating grin on his face.

"You wrong for that man, she seems cool."

Both men sat slumped over in their chairs like they were just seconds away from falling asleep.

"You know why they make you wait in these soft ass chairs don't you?" Melvin asked an already half dozed Dave.

"Why is that my brotha?"

"It's because they know… they know that you don't know what the fuck you're sittin' out here for, and this chair helps your ass pucker up without any resistance, that's why!"

Dave had closed his eyes completely at this point and only grunted in response to what he considered was more bullshit from Mel.

A soft buzz sounded from the young lady's phone. She pushed a button on the phone panel and spoke into the phone directly.

"Yes Mr. Kohl?" she answered with that cigarette and gin voice. "Right away sir."

She depressed the button and stood up.

"You may go in now Mr. Dossier."

Melvin glanced over at Dave, nudged his arm then whispered, "You waitin' here man?" Dave slowly got up.

"Didn't I tell you that I've got your back? How am I gone have your back from out here? I can't cut a motha fucka from out here man. Now come on, let's go get some!"

"You've got some anger management issues bro. You really need to seek some kind of help or get you some ass or somethin'."

Dave looked at Melvin, adjusted his jacket and they headed toward the door of Mr. Kohl's office.

Just as the men approached the shiny cherry wood door, it slowly opened. There, in the doorway, stood a silver haired man with a full silver beard. He was small in stature, but was very confident looking. His pinstriped gray suit was cut to perfection. His shirt was crisp, and his tie even had one of those gold pins with the little chain attached. Oh yeah, he looked like a man in charge.

The little man stuck out his hand and shook Melvin's hand, saying in a cheery voice, "Come right in gentlemen, come right in."

He then reached over and shook Dave's hand while introducing himself as Mr. Kohl. He directed both men to the chairs in front of his desk.

Both men walked over to the desk while looking around.

"Man, this is a nice office. How much you pullin' in a year up in here Jack?" Dave tactlessly asked.

Melvin cleared his throat and nudged Dave. Mr. Kohl ignored the question. He stepped just outside of his office and asked the receptionist to hold all of his calls. He then closed his door and walked over to a small file cabinet that sat just under the office window.

The window overlooked Pennsylvania Avenue and provided a colorful view of the Virginia side of the Memorial Bridge.

He glanced out of the window for a second then bent over and opened the cabinet and flipped a few folders back.

"Ah, here we are."

He pulled out a brown folder, you know the kind that you always see in those spy movies with the rubber bands tied around them. Well, this one didn't have a rubber band, but it did have some spy looking documents in it.

"Do you know why you're here Mr. Dossier?"

Melvin looked down at the folder, and then over at Dave.

"Well, I was hopin' you could tell me," he answered while adjusting the knot of his kangaroo tie.

Mr. Kohl opened up the folder and pulled out several documents and an envelope. He also pulled a big metal instrument over towards him and some other papers that he had on top of the same file cabinet.

"Mr. Dossier, I hate to be the one to inform you but…,"

Dave sat up in his chair and mumbled, "Aww shit, here it comes!"

Mr. Kohl glanced over at Dave and then continued, "Mr. Dossier, your uncle, Cleveland T. Salter has passed on. With his passing, he left you all of his assets."

Melvin sat in the chair quietly then started rubbing his face with his right hand while staring down at the floor.

"What the fu… ?" Melvin whispered. "I don't get it. I don't get it at all. The man didn't even like me. Well at least I thought he didn't, maybe I was wrong."

Just then Melvin heard a soft voice just over his left shoulder, "All I want to know is, was the motha fucka rich? Sheeeeeit!"

Mr. Kohl picked up the letter that was in the folder and placed it down in front of Melvin.

"This is for you, from your uncle."

Melvin picked it up and looked at the front of the envelope. It read:

"To Melvin, My Nephew"

Melvin opened up the envelope and pulled out the letter, and began to read:

Melvin,

I am writing this letter to you because you are my last surviving relative. I would rather leave all my shit to you than to have my shit go to the state, 'cause you know what kind of greedy mother fuckers they are. Enjoy my shit, even though you've never done shit to deserve my shit. Melvin, I've never really liked your ass. I never thought that you would ever amount to be worth a piece of shit hanging from the tip of my ass. I knew you wouldn't amount to shit, and always thought you would grow up to be full of shit just like your daddy who aint worth a shit. You lucked up boy, and if I find out some how that you sold my shit, I'm gonna haunt your ass. And in the event I get resurrected, I want my shit back. My nephew Melvin, I loved your mother, Baby Sis, dearly. She was a sweet woman, God rest her soul. So I guess I should clear the air between you and me since the time has come for me. I never had a chance to tell you this, so now is as good a time as any. No, fuck that shit. I can't tell that lie, not even in death. As far as I'm concerned, you can KISS MY ASS, and eat shit!

Fuck You,
Uncle Cleve

Melvin folded the letter and slipped it back into the envelope. He stared at the floor as if he was so touched by the letter, but it was only to hide the embarrassment and hatred that he still had for his uncle. Melvin had always considered him to be a pure and true asshole and even though he knew that his uncle Cleve was an arrogant bastard, he was still hurt by his letter.

"Do you need a moment?" Mr. Kohl asked.

Melvin slowly looked up and shook his head, "No, no let's continue."

"My man!" Came the whisper from just over Melvin's left shoulder.

"Are you sure Mr. Dossier? I'm sure that this is quite a shock for you. If you'd like to reschedule this meeting for later this week, that's understandable." Mr. Kohl asked now appearing to be really concerned.

"HELL NO! I mean, uh no. That will be quite alright. There's no need to prolong this. The sooner all of this is done, the better. I'm sure that my uncle would want that. Rest his soul. I'm truly gonna miss him."

After listening to Melvin put on this song and dance, Dave belted out a loud chuckle. Mr. Kohl glared over at Dave which caused Melvin to do the same. After noticing both men staring at him, Dave began tapping on his chest with his fist then mumbled.

"Excuse me fellas, it's just gas."

Mr. Kohl turned from Dave. He moved some of the materials lying on the desk to the side in preparation for Melvin's documents.

"As you wish, Mr. Dossier."

Mr. Kohl began pulling the other papers from the folder and explaining what each document was. He showed Melvin where to sign and then would take the metal device from the side of his desk and stamped each document with it. Melvin continued to sign the documents, and then Mr. Kohl spoke those magical words.

"So, where would you like your money sent? We can wire it anywhere you'd like."

Melvin sat up in the chair and tried to keep from smiling. He was ready to explode with excitement. If there was a large enough piece of cardboard lying on the floor, he probably would have jumped up and started break dancing. Can you imagine, Fat boy spinning around on a piece of cardboard in that tight jacket? He still couldn't believe that he had finally gotten a break. Especially from his hated Uncle Cleve.

He sat there thinking about what he could do with some real money. He thought about buying a new car, a nice place to live, women, and most of all, food. As he was clearing his mind from those things in order to move along with the business at hand, he noticed a slight bulge in his pants. Yes, Melvin was starting to get an erection. The bad part of it all is that he wasn't sure if he was getting a woody from thinking of being surrounded by beautiful women or being surrounded by scrumptious foods. Then he thought, "What am I thinking about? Uncle Cleve was not a rich man. He was crazy and weird, but rich, hell nah."

Melvin's mind soon left the yacht and the women. He started thinking more about using the money to get the Escort fixed and maybe updating his wardrobe.

Melvin gently tapped the desk with the thick gold and black "Cross" brand ink pen that Mr. Kohl had let him use to sign the documents with, which by the way, he had already made up in his mind to steal during his office departure. Yep, Melvin was just that ghetto, still with rotten bastard-type thoughts running through his head. He didn't know yet that he could buy as many of those pens as he wanted. Of course, we know he's not the sharpest knife in the drawer, and probably has the IQ of a salad bar, but come on, a pen?

After a few seconds, Melvin stood up and produced a folded up piece of ashy black leather that was held together with black electrician's tape, which contained pictures, expired credit cards, business cards, and small pieces of paper crammed inside. He dug through this mini file cabinet while pressing his tongue against the corner of his mouth.

"Here it is. You can send the money to this account."

Mr. Kohl wrote the account number down on one of the documents and passed the damp crumpled up card back to Melvin. Melvin slipped the sweaty card back into his wallet and placed both of his forearms on the desk.

"Is that it?" Melvin asked while scratching his head.

Mr. Kohl gathered all of the documents and stood up extending his hand to Melvin.

"That's it Mr. Dossier. I'll be transferring the 1.6 million dollars to that account first thing in the morning."

Melvin and Dave's mouths flung open simultaneously, "One point six? One point six mil?" Dave shouted.

Mr. Kohl smiled at Melvin, and in a calm voice said, "Yes, yes Mr. Dossier along with the Mount Vernon home where he resided. With the sales of his trucking business and his beach house just before he passed, your uncle had quite a nest egg, and now that nest egg belongs to you."

Both Melvin and Dave sat back down and stared out of the window, the same way they did on most evenings, but today was different. Today there was no weed involved. Melvin was really in deep thought now. Now his visions of yachts, music video dancers, and catered buffets were running through his mind once again. Finally both men got up and shook Mr. Kohl's hand again.

Mr. Kohl, looking at Melvin, had a strange look on his face. "Are you alright Mr. Dossier?"

"I'm still in shock, but that's a lot to take in. Wow! I don't think I've ever been this excited."

Mr. Kohl positioned himself in front of his office door and whispered to Melvin, "Well you might want to take a few minutes and unexcite yourself just a little. We don't want to get my secretary too worked up now, do we?"

Confused, Melvin looked at Mr. Kohl. Mr. Kohl looked at Melvin, and then slowly moved his eyes down Melvin's body until he reached his crotch area.

"Damn man, what the hell?" Dave yelled out while shielding his eyes. Melvin looked down at the stretched fabric of his trousers. His member was harder than a ten-cent chisel.

"Oh my damn! I guess I got a little too excited. You know, what with the money and all. Sorry about that."

"It's quite alright Mr. Dossier. It happens, but you might want to tuck it away before you leave here, or maybe hang around until you can deflate this situation?"

The men chuckled. They stood there in the office for another ten minutes trying to discuss any topic that would calm Melvin down. Melvin, still with a look of shock on his face somehow managed to shrink his bulge and headed for the door without uttering another word.

After leaving Mr. Kohl's office, the men walked past the receptionist without even acknowledging her.

"Have a nice day gentlemen," she said, but they walked right by as if they were zombies.

Neither man spoke a word until they reached the lobby. Oh and by the way, Melvin still stole Mr. Kohl's pen.

"I gotta piss," Melvin mumbled with that blank look on his face, and then headed for the men's room.

Dave walked outside, pulled out his cell phone and leaned against the wall while he waited. On Melvin's return from the men's room, the security guard rose from her seat and walked from behind the large desk.

"Sir, I would like to once again apologize for the misunderstanding earlier."

Melvin, still in his daze, nodded his head and continued walking toward the doors. As he neared the guard she extended her hand out in his direction. Melvin, now looking beyond the woman, continued on. He hadn't noticed that in her hand, was a small piece of paper with her phone number written on it. He walked right by her. As he was just about to exit the doors, he could hear her faint voice in the distance.

"Whatever, with that tight ass suit on!"

CHAPTER 4   THE WIRE

After Melvin's return, both men still remained quiet as the parking attendant pulled up with their car. They got in the Escort and drove down 12th Street.

"DROP DOWN AND GET YOUR EAGLE ON, DROP DOWN AND GET YOUR EAGLE ON," Nelly sang from inside the Dave-loaned suit jacket that Melvin was wearing. Melvin reached in the inside pocket of the suit and pulled out his black bootleg Cingular Razor cell phone.

The ring tone blared out even louder now, "DROP DOWN AND GET… "

"Yeah? Who dis? Uh huh, what the… how'd you? I don't believe this shit!"

Melvin flipped the phone shut and looked over at Dave who was now glancing casually out of the car window. It seems that while Melvin was in the men's room, Mr. Dave had made a few calls informing a few neighborhood friends of Melvin's good fortune.

"Why man? You know they gone be on me like stink on shit! You know how the wire is around the way."

Melvin continued to yell at him, but Dave just kept looking out the window.

"I couldn't help it man, I got excited and it just slipped out. Damn, my bad."

Dave turned and looked at Melvin; he had a big bright smile on his face.

"Hey man, you know what?"

Melvin kept looking at the road and frowned up his mouth before answering, "What?"

"I know one thing's for sure Mel."

"And what might that be genius?"

Dave slid down in his seat grabbing his crotch with his left hand and pumping the fist of his right hand in the air.

"We gone get higher than an NBA player's child support tonight boy! And some lucky young lady is gonna be pointin' her toes to the stars ALL night!"

"All night? You must be plannin' on pullin' out that blow up doll you keep hidden under your bed tonight then. Look, this is me man, I've seen you in action. I know after your measly two minutes of fake studsmanship the only lady whose toes will be pointin' to the stars would be that of Becky Blow-Up! And that's only 'cause she's stuck in that position, Grand Master Flash."

"Man you must be trippin'! Boy, they call me Dave the Wave, 'cause they know I'll roll up in that ass all night long!"

"Yeah, you're just like a wave, too. Roll up all fast, then splash! And you know what? It don't even matter man, you know why?"

"Why is that?"

Melvin looked over at Dave, then yelled at the top of his voice, "'CAUSE, I'M RICH BEEEEOTCH!"

Both men laughed, yelled, and sang in celebration as they made their way back home.

They pulled up slowly to the vacant curbside parking space in front of Dave's building. Melvin had his right arm slung across the passenger seat as he began backing into the space. Then he stopped the car and looked at Dave.

"See, what'd I tell you? They're like roaches right after the lights turn out! Hell, you might as well have announced it on a damn loud speaker!"

Dave turned to look behind the car and coming from all over, were people who wanted to congratulate Melvin. Well, maybe not congratulate him, but at least find out for themselves how much money he got and how much of it they could get.

"Five seconds after I get out, I'll become the Money Store. Watch."

Melvin continued parking, waving at the group of people and displaying a fake grin. He turned the engine off, and they got out.

As soon as Melvin stepped on to the sidewalk, Tyrone, one of the neighborhood junkies, approached him.

"Watcha gone do with this car now that you're a big balla Mel? You may as well pass them keys right on over to me now bro 'cause I know you gone git yo self a Benz or somethin' hot like that." The man said jokingly.

"For what? All you gone do is fuck it up with your non-drivin' ass! This is a precision automobile! Take your beggin' ass back in the house anyway. You'll just get all high and tear it up, damn junkie. Now move out of the way!" Dave yelled at the man as he continued walking towards him.

The man's big grin shriveled up as he turned and walked away. Tyrone didn't want to have anything to do with Dave. He knew that Dave would not hesitate to beat him down if he spoke another word. Dave turned around and walked back over and leaned towards Melvin who was just standing around slapping high fives to everybody.

"You're gonna have to say somethin' to these motha fuck-as to get them out the way or we'll be out here all day."

Melvin nodded in agreement, and then yelled out, "Oh we gone party tomorrow night at The Sapphire y'all. Be there. Men come to party, and women hell, you can just come to cum! Drinks are on me! Put on your best shit, too. Ladies don't come up in there with half of your ass hangin' out and fellas no gym shit. You wanna work out, stay your ass home. If that's all you have to wear, stay your ass home. Now make a hole people and let me through."

Everybody cheered as Melvin and Dave weaved their way towards Dave's place. Midway through the crowd their path was obstructed. Now standing in front of Melvin was Larry in all his splendor. He stood there tall in his tight jeans, Prince-like high-heeled purple pleather boots, and tank top with a cut off sweat-shirt covering half his stomach. His hair draped past his shoul-ders and he had his hands on his hips.

"Melvin, you're so generous. I'm so happy for you. This couldn't have happened to a nicer person. I still remember when we used to play together when we were kids. You remember how we used to wrestle?"

Everybody knew Larry's story and Melvin didn't want to become one of the chapters.

"Man, I don't remember that shit. I remember you being the hopscotch champ of the neighborhood and you jumpin' rope with the girls most of the time, pissin' them off makin' them turn double-dutch for you all damn day. You always threatened to kick their asses if they didn't turn for you. You were a jumpin' fool, too. Damn man, is that a weave?"

Larry looked at Melvin with attitude. He was somewhat flustered by feeling insulted and complimented at the same time.

"Melly, you know I got Indian in my blood. Both my par-ents are half Indian."

"So that's your real hair huh? Cool. Oh yeah, I can see the Indian now."

Larry rolled his eyes turned up his nose and strutted off in his high heeled boots. Dave looked at Melvin who was grinning hard and trying not to explode from holding in his laughter.

"You really used to wrestle with Larry?"

"Man whatever. Talkin' bout his daddy's Indian. He must be from the "Hum-a-Nut" tribe."

"Yeah, I can see that now. A bunch of Indians with pink feathers and headbands, mini loincloths, leg warmers and mocca-sins with six-inch heels made from tree bark. Dancin' around the fire, instead of pattin' their mouths yellin' 'woo, woo … woo … woo', they'd have their hands cupped like they were holdin' dicks poppin' those holes against their lips chantin', 'oh, ahh … hmmm … ahh … hmmm … oh … yummm', then stopping to Vogue."

"Ha! Yeah, and probably ridin' ponies, too. You know, as I look out into the crowd here, I see countless numbers of 'Hum-a-Nut' tribal descendants. Damn, and Dana over there has to be a direct descendant of the chief 'cause you know how she rolls. Now that girl can probably suck a golf ball through a garden hose. She's the only woman that I know has a PHD in 'Headsmanship'. I aint gone lie, I bought some of that head a couple of times myself. She can tomahawk these nuts anytime, Ha!"

"Sure you're right! Donald was just tellin' me the other day how she had just scalped his nuts! Left 'em bald and drained."

The men broke out into heavy laughter. No one in the crowd had any idea what they were so amused by, but it was contagious. Soon everyone surrounding them was engrossed in laughter.

"Man, forget that mess. You really gonna buy drinks for all those freeloadin' crack smokin' junkies? I mean these are some of the same ruthless motha fucka's, who'll drink up your money, beg for a loan that they never intend to pay back, then steal your damn car to get back home. Man, fuck them! These are some of the same bastards that stole your caps off your car man and if permitted enough time, would have snatched the tires as well. Come on man!"

Melvin looked at Dave and shook his head in disgust.

"See? That's what's wrong with the world. Don't you have any heart at all? These are our people and no matter how ruthless some of these assholes are, I grew up with most of them. And you know the deal; I just might need one of these fools later on to cut the grass or wash my Bentley or somethin'. Just because I'm rich now, doesn't mean I'll lose my hustlin' game. I mean, cheap labor is cheap labor. I could probably get one of these crackheads to catch the bus to my house, cut the grass, wash the car, and paint the outside of my house for four dollars.

Wait a minute… what's crack pussy goin' for these days, four, five bucks? Okay, well make that cut, wash, and paint for about ten bucks. Besides, look at some of the ladies out there lookin' all pitiful and shit. They're just beggin' to give some of that ass up man. I can see at least a couple of long lost blow jobs out there."

Dave looked back into the growing group of neighbors. He reached over and placed his hand on Melvin's shoulder and grinned.

"Always' thinkin' my man! Always thinkin'! You know, even in the biggest pile of dog shit, you can find a quarter. You've got an ingenious mind man. You're right! That's a sea of head out there, crackhead, but hey, head is head. I'd let 'em all do me, too. Well, probably not that one over there diggin' in her crotch. Who is that, Regina? What in the hell is she lookin' to find in there? What ever it is, it's either acidified, rusted, or smells really nasty. That bitch is about to burn her damn nails off. I bet that snatch smells worse than her breath, too. You ever smelled that shit? Her breath always smells like she's been lickin' feet! You need two mints for her stank breath, one for each of your nostrils. Then, she's always got that white shit around her mouth. She might have a yeast infection in there, too."

"Damn, I don't know man. Maybe she's bakin' bread up in that cat with all that yeast."

Both men frowned up their faces as they watched the young woman scratch continuously in her genital area.

Melvin placed his hand over his mouth while placing his thumb and index finger against his nostrils, "Damn, all I know is, I aint never eatin' bread again!" His muffled words pushed through his blocked mouth.

"That's why I stick to head with the neighborhood nasties. You just can't take a chance hittin' them man. You'll be walkin' down the street and your dick'll just fall right down your pant leg and on to the sidewalk or you'll go to piss one day and your dick'll just crush up in your hands from bein' decayed from the inside out."

"I've changed my mind about these hos. I think we ought to go pull some of the clean tramps from The Sapphire tonight. You gotta con these hos into gettin' naked, but hey, I'll do what I gotta do to hit somethin' whose ass won't burn through a condom. Yeah, I think that's a better plan."

Dave reached out and pulled open the glass door which led to his building. He nodded in agreement and pointed up the stairs.

"Let's go roll a few to celebrate. And as always, my treat! You think maybe now that you have some dough, you can spring for some get high sometimes?"

"Hell no, you're the man, remember?"

The guys headed upstairs without looking back at the still celebrating crowd.

CHAPTER 5   NOTHING TO LOSE

The sun seemed extra bright this morning for Melvin. He was extremely hung over from all the private celebrating that he and Dave had done the night before. He managed to roll himself over and prop himself up against the headboard of his bed. He pushed a half empty bottle of Budweiser over to the other side of his nightstand, placed both hands on his knees, closed his eyes and then dropped his head.

After sitting there for over fifteen minutes, he clumsily staggered into his bathroom and turned the water on in the shower. After a quick shower, Melvin slipped on his underwear, walked over to his dirty laundry basket and pulled out the coordinated ensemble for the day; gray sweatpants and his favorite Malcolm X tee shirt. He then dug deeper into the basket to retrieve two dingy off white sweat socks. He slipped on his pants then his shirt then plopped down on the closed toilet seat. He grunted and strained for a minute or two until he was finally able to lift his ankle onto his opposite knee. Realizing that he was holding two mismatched socks in each hand, he continued to place the dull, worn stocking onto his foot. After dropping his leg, he repeated his grunting and straining technique until both feet were covered.

Melvin returned to his room and slowly lowered himself down until he was on both knees. He reached under the bed to retrieve the one low top "All Star Converse" basketball shoe that he had noticed as he returned from the bathroom. He pulled himself up and sat on the side of the bed and slipped his foot into the shoe only to realize that it would need to be tied. Melvin looked around the room, never leaving his position on the soft bed. His head was still pounding. He finally spotted the other dusty white rubber bottomed shoe lying beside his dresser. He sat still for another minute hoping that somehow the shoe would realize that he needed it and float its way over. The shoe never moved. Melvin got up, moaning. Now the gas was kicking in as well. He knew the diarrhea was soon to follow. He made his way over to the still motionless shoe. Placing the toes of his right foot inside the heel portion of the shoe, he managed to extract it from its resting place. He stood wiggling and stomping and shoving his foot inside the shoe until his foot was snugly wedged inside with the tongue of the shoe imbedded deep beyond the opening.

Melvin, not wanting to bend over and spill the remaining fragments of his brain onto the floor stood trying to think. He did not want to go through the trouble of trying to maneuver his ankles over those trunks that he called thighs, or lowering himself and not being able to get back up again. He stood thinking as hard as he could. Minutes had passed as he stood still trying to think. All he could hear was the small hum, a faint kind of buzzing with a high pitch. Then he realized that he wasn't thinking at all. His ears were ringing from the re-construction work being performed in his head.

Melvin then did what any red blooded human being would do. He stuck the front of his left shoe on the back of the right shoe and snatched his foot out. After removing both shoes, walked over to his closet and slipped his feet into his run over heeled loafers. He stood looking at the dull white socks crunched up and protruding over the top of his shoe. He wiggled his toes to try to relieve their confinement then rocked back on the almost vacant heels. Realizing that he was looking like a hot mess, he made a few adjustments by tucking in his shirt and tightening the drawstring of his sweatpants. He looked once more at the shoes then snatched his shirt back out and grunted, "Fuck it!"

Still holding his pounding head, he tipped into the kitchen and retrieved a bottle of "Excedrin" aspirin from the cabinet above the refrigerator. He opened the refrigerator door and grabbed the bottle of draft beer that sat alone on the top rack, twisted off the top, popped the aspirin in his mouth and gulped down half of the cold beer. He quietly closed the refrigerator door, turned, grabbed his keys and his wallet and headed out the door. That's when it hit.

He felt a rumble in his stomach that he truly thought was demonic. He rushed back inside and ran through the living room throwing his keys onto the couch. He ran in the bathroom, pulling and tugging on the string to his sweatpants. He yanked several times, but his sweats stayed put. The string was knotted. Melvin was now beginning to perspire.

"Oh damn!"

He tried squeezing his buttocks past the tightly tied string, but it would not give. Now vigorously pacing from door to tub, Melvin was in a panic. He could visualize the wet hot brown sponge like substance running down his leg. He quickly opened the medicine cabinet. Lying on the bottom shelf, he saw his manicure kit and grabbed it. He opened it up and pulled out the nail clipper. He tried clipping at the nylon string but it was useless. It was too thick for the small opening on the clippers. Melvin quickly threw the clippers down on the sink and grabbed the scissors out of the kit. He could no longer concentrate.

He continued his pacing until he was able to stand still for a brief moment. He stuck the nylon string between the two sharp blades of the scissors and began to squeeze. He repeated this several more times. The string was not cutting. Melvin had no choice, his rear muscles were beginning to weaken. The small opening that he was holding together so tightly was loosening its seal. Just then, Melvin reached behind him and pulled the fabric of his sweatpants away from his body. He took the scissors and cut down the stitching in the back of his pants. He repeated this hacking on his underwear. Then he dropped the scissors and with both hands reached back and ripped opened his garments. There was a loud tear.

Melvin plopped down onto the toilet and gripped tightly on to the sink in front of him. Splat! He let go. He was perspiring more than ever now. His insides seemed to flow endlessly. He could hear the splash and popping echo over his sighs. It was warm. Melvin was now feeling so relieved. It was like ecstasy.

"Ahhhhhh yeah. Thank you, thank you, thank you," he whispered.

The walls resembled a cheap oil painting of a pastel blue sky with greenish brown clouds. From a bird's eye view, he saw images of tiny islands surrounded by a polluted sea over the ceramic tiled floor. That's when he realized that he never lifted the toilet seat lid after putting on his socks that morning. As he emptied all of his bowels, they splattered throughout the small room. Melvin stood up slowly and looked around. There was wet feces sliding slowly down the back and one of the side walls and left splattered splotches on the floor.

"Awwww shit! What the fuck? How in the hell did I do that? Damn it Melvin, you stupid ass!? Now I've got to clean up all this crap. Damn! Damn! Damn! This shit stinks, too. Ah it stinks! What a way to start your fuckin' mornin'!"

Angrily, Melvin slowly unglued his thighs and buttocks from the toilet seat lid. He felt just plain nasty. He backed up to the tub and pulled his washcloth from off the rack. His head was no longer aching, nor was he perspiring any longer, but he was reeking of the warm stench that had just erupted out of his body.

Melvin stood there and washed his backside until there were no more signs of the brown matter. He tiptoed out of the bathroom into the kitchen where he grabbed a steak knife out of the utensil drawer and cut the string from his sweatpants. Now free, he pulled out a white plastic trash bag from under the kitchen sink and threw in the stained ripped garments.

After returning to the bathroom, now with bucket and mop, he began to remove his mess from the walls and cleaned the floor. The stench hung in the air, like an endless thick fog that you couldn't seem to get through. It sat on his face like a horny college freshman girl and wouldn't let go.

After scrubbing and mopping for over an hour, Melvin jumped into the shower and returned to his hamper. He grabbed another pair of pants and some socks then returned to his room and retrieved a pair of shoes from deep in the back of his closet that he hadn't worn in years. He wasn't about to clean those shoes that he knew he'd probably never wear again. After all, he's rich.

Now even more dehydrated, he stopped in the kitchen, stuck his head under the faucet and ran some water into his mouth. What'd you expect, a glass? He looked at his watch, grabbed his keys from off the couch and headed out the door once again.

Melvin arrived at work late as ever. He didn't care. He didn't check the time cards, didn't check the mail bins, he didn't even scan through the sorted mail to see what could accidentally get opened. Nope, he just went straight downstairs to the snack bar to buy his usual hot cup of coffee and a jumbo honey bun.

"Thank you and have a wonderful day," Melvin said as he paid the clerk for his breakfast. For the first time ever, he even dropped his spare pennies from his change into the white ceramic coffee mug that sat next to the cash register. The clerk, Mr. Powell, looked as if he were in shock.

Mr. Powell, the old Vietnam veteran and resident expert on all subjects, was one of Melvin's least favorite people there. He always had a smart remark for anyone that stepped into his establishment. He was just one of those angry, negative people who wanted everyone to be as unhappy as he appeared to be. Limping about with the use of his prosthetic leg and mumbling to himself most times, lead everyone to believe that he wasn't quite right in the head.

Every morning he would force feed his patrons with his abundance of knowledge on any topic that he overheard them discussing as they walked in or crammed one of his war stories down their ears until they were able to break free. It got so bad that most of the people in there wouldn't talk at all the entire time they were in the snack bar. They would just pickup what they needed, pay and leave hoping not to spark any conversation from the old guy.

On those unfortunate occasions when his patrons would get caught, he would sometimes lecture them on the contents of food and how poisonous it was to the human body. Food that he sold, now how stupid is that? Buy a diet soda and the first thing you'd hear is, "You know them thangs got aspartame in 'em, it'll kill ya, kill ya dead it will."

Buy a pack of gum and you're going to hear, "Say, you know how much sugar's in this stuff? It'll kill ya, kill ya dead it will."

Mr. Powell would talk and make comments to everybody who crossed his threshold, everybody except Melvin. Every time Melvin would walk in, Mr. Powell would push up his blue and gold "VFW" cap and start reading the newspaper just to ignore him. He still had a chip on his shoulder ever since that morning he and Melvin had crossed paths. You see, one morning Melvin bought his usual morning jolt of coffee and jumbo honey bun. Mr. Powell thought that he'd let him know just how unhealthy his breakfast was. Melvin walked in and grabbed his bun and asked for a cup of coffee.

"You know this stuff is goin' to kill you one of these days. That honey bun is full of cholesterol. Do you know what kind of damage this can do to your heart? Kill ya dead it will."

Melvin paid Mr. Powell, picked up his coffee and started toward the counter.

"And that coffee, well you know what caffeine will do to ya, kill ya dead man, kill ya dead."

Melvin looked down and slowly pulled out his underwear that was wedged deeply in the crevasse of his rear. He raised his head slowly and pointed to Mr. Powell.

"Shut the hell up why don't you? Every mornin' it's the same old crap!"

This particular morning Melvin was just not up to listening to Mr. Powell's negativities. Some say he had women problems during that time. Some say he was having serious financial issues, but whatever he was going through, it was just the wrong time for Mr. Powell's suggestions.

"Do YOU know what kind of damage a pissed off man my size will do to your ass? Kill ya I will, kill ya dead I will. Damn hypocrite, don't sell this shit if you think it's harmful to folks then. As a matter of fact, either turn this dump into a health food store or shut the fuck up! I don't see your ass over there suckin' on alfalfa sprouts. And what's that's you're sippin' on? Bean curd? Hell nah, it's coffee damn it! So shut the hell up you fake ass VFW war reject bastard!"

Mr. Powell became furious and slammed both his fists down on the counter making a thunderous thud.

"Boy you don't know nuthin' bout me! I served this country. I lost a leg for this country! What you know 'bout discipline, code, honor, or respect Boy?"

Melvin walked slowly toward the counter.

"Man, go on with that! What you know 'bout that? Huh? You got that crap off of the movie *A Few Good Men*. Yeah, I saw it, too! And I know you don't know a damn thing about it, either. You see, I know Ms. Taylor. Oh, don't look shocked like you don't know. Yes, I know Big Shirley Taylor, and Ms. Taylor knows you! Now when she found out that I was workin' here, she told me all about you. How you lost your leg over forty years ago workin' for the railroad and how you always wanted to be in the service like your buddies and how jealous you were of them because you wanted to be the big war hero. How you used to listen to her brother's war stories and how this here is the only job that you could get. Says you got a little money from the accident, but blew that on the ponies and casinos."

Melvin inched a little closer to the now sheepish looking clerk and started to speak to him in a calm voice.

"So look here, if you want to keep your little secret safe: whenever you see me walk in here, just pour my damn coffee and KEEP YOUR DAMN MOUTH SHUT!"

Mr. Powell stood glaring at Melvin with his fists still balled.

"So what, you constipated? You must be, 'cause I know you're not swellin' up on me old man!" Melvin started to shout. "Hell, you can bring your ass right on 'round that counter. Oh hell yeah, I'll fight an old man! I'll rip off that bad leg of yours and pop you right in your eye wit it then break the rest off in your ass. You'll be a one legged, popped eye, ass splintered, wooden foot hangin' out your ass havin', bean curd sippin' ass bastard when I'm through! Don't tempt me old man, not today!"

After seeing just how angry Melvin was, Mr. Powell thought that maybe, just maybe, it would be in his best interest to lean back against the counter and read the morning paper and just keep quiet. Melvin left quietly.

From that day to this, neither Mr. Powell nor Melvin had ever spoken one word to each other. That's why Mr. Powell couldn't believe that Melvin had actually acknowledged him after all this time. Melvin, ever so happy, continued to smile as he unwrapped his huge lump of cholesterol filled sugar bread. He inhaled a big bite and headed for the condiments. He pulled the lid off of the smoking coffee cup and placed it on the counter. He grabbed six of the small white and blue packets of sugar substitute from the square metal container and ripped them open two at a time. After pouring all of the packets into his java, Melvin reached over the napkins and pulled out three of the stirrers from the plastic cup and four small sealed cups of cream from a similar metal container that was half filled with melted ice. Melvin started peeling the lid from each of the containers of cream one by one, pouring each one into his beverage and then shooting the empty containers into the trashcan as if he were standing at the foul line of a basketball court.

Mr. Powell continued to watch Melvin as each empty container fell to the floor, one by one. Melvin then devoured the remaining chunk of his honey bun. He took the sticky wrapper and balled it up and spun around and attempted his best jump shot. The wrapper bounced off the trashcan, ricocheted off the back wall, and landed in the potato chip bin.

"Not quite NBA material, are we?" Mr. Powell just couldn't resist. He just had to say something since Melvin had finally broken their silence.

Melvin looked up at him and smiled. "I could have made that shot back in the day but you know, after I blew my knee out, you know how it goes, my game just kinda went downhill."

"Well you don't look like you've ever been in any real kind of athletic type of condition." Mr. Powell mumbled.

"What? What the hell did you say? You see? That's exactly what I mean. You try to be nice and some people still have to act like jackasses. But you know what? Not even a clown like you can steal my joy today, fool. You have a great day!"

Melvin started towards the door. Just as he passed through the archway he stopped. He slowly turned towards Mr. Powell and clicked his heels together and then rendered him a stiff salute.

"Choo! Choooooo!" Melvin sang out.

"You son of a bitch." Mr. Powell grunted.

Now laughing loudly, Melvin left the snack bar and made his way back upstairs to the mail counter and sat sipping coffee from his cup. With a huge smile on his face, Melvin was still thinking about how lucky he was and how pissed off Mr. Powell was.

"You'll never accomplish anything by just sitting there young man. Don't you think there's something worthwhile that you could be doing this morning?"

Melvin turned and looked over his left shoulder and dropped his smile. It was Mr. Carr, one of the VPs who always treated everyone as if they were beneath him. He acted as if every dime made for the company was his doing, and every dime lost came directly out of his own pocket. The mailroom peasants were scum in his eyes.

Melvin stared at Mr. Carr, turned back around in the chair and kept sipping his coffee.

"Did you hear me young man?" Mr. Carr shouted.

"Damn, what a mornin' this is turnin' out to be. Two ass-holes in one day," Melvin thought to himself.

Melvin stood up, placed his cup of coffee back on the counter and walked over to Mr. Carr. With his smile reappearing on his face, Melvin spoke slowly in a monotone voice, "Yeah, I got somethin' I could be doin'. How bout I stick my foot so deep up in yo ass that next week, your breath will still smell like the dog shit that I stepped in this mornin'?"

Mr. Carr stood there in shock.

"How dare you? How dare you address me in that manner?"

Melvin could tell that Mr. Carr was feeling a little intimidated. Melvin stood even closer, "I'll address your ass any way I damn well please. As a matter of fact, not only will I address you, but I'll undress you and have your punk ass runnin' around this building buck ass naked like the little bitch that you are!"

Mr. Carr slowly backed away from Melvin and whispered just loud enough for Melvin to hear.

"He's gone postal. I'm getting security."

Melvin walked in the back and grabbed the mail cart destined for the seventh floor.

"I've got seven!" Melvin yelled, and headed for the elevator.

Once upstairs, Melvin headed straight for Wendy's desk. She looked up and saw him approaching just as she was pushing herself up from her desk to stand.

"Well, if it isn't the Campbell's soup man himself. So what do you want today? You don't have enough to do down there in the dungeon with the rest of the critters?"

She gathered up some papers from her cluttered desk and headed toward the Xerox machine, which was located in a small room across the hall from her desk.

"Class. C'mon Mel, think of somethin' classy to say to this ho. Damn that, I'm rich now. I can find another one that looks just like her." Melvin thought just before yelling out.

"You won't be talkin' that shit for long woman!" He followed her in to the Xerox room and continued bragging.

"That's right! I know you heard. I'm 'bout to get paid girl, big time, too. You haven't gotten the 411? Girl, you better ask somebody! As a matter of fact, I don't even need this stank job no more either! So what you gone do? You gone get on the bus before it starts rollin' or are you gone miss it? Girl you're lookin' at a millionaire! Did you hear me? A millionaire! After today, I'll be the best dressed brotha you know and if you act right, I might even take you to an island or two."

Wendy placed her papers in the slot, and pushed a few buttons until the machine started. She turned and looked him up and down then walked up to him, leaned over and placed her cheek against his.

"Is that a piece of bacon stuck in your teeth?" then turned and walked out the door.

Melvin stood for a second digging in his gap, until he realized that he hadn't even eaten any bacon this morning. Melvin walked out of the noisy room wiping the spit from his finger down the side of his shirt. Wendy had just picked up her phone, which had been ringing as she was approaching her desk.

"What? Really? You're kidding me," Wendy spoke into the phone as she looked away from Melvin.

"Oh now she's findin' out the real deal. Somebody's fillin' her in," Melvin thought to himself. "Now her tone will change, but now I'll play the role. I'll let her kiss my ass for a change. Yeah, she'll be beggin' me to holla at her now. I'm just gone play it cool and have her follow me back into the Xerox room and show me those titties."

Melvin stopped in front of Wendy's desk and placed both hands on the edge of the glass top of her desk. He poked out his chest and looked down at her. She looked up at Melvin from her desk.

"Oh, you're still here?"

"That's all you gotta say huh? I know you know what's up. Well just don't be tryin' to holler at a brotha after you get the real '411' either. All I'm sayin' is that you'd betta recognize girl."

Melvin grabbed the cart, which was still full of the morning mail, which he had no intention of delivering, and stormed off.

"Hey Melvin!"

Melvin stopped and slowly turned around trying to hold in his grin. "I got her ass now," he thought.

Wendy motioned him over to her desk. Melvin left the cart up against the wall and strutted back over to Wendy. She stood up. Melvin stared at her legs and for the first time she smiled at Melvin. She motioned Melvin closer. Melvin leaned over the desk as she met him half way.

She placed her soft lips against Melvin's ear and whispered, "Hey Mel, let me be the first to tell you: you look like shit today. You'll probably look like shit tomorrow, too. Best dressed? Are those 'Earthshoes' you're wearing? Where in the hell did you find a pair of those? Wait. Don't tell me. I really don't want to know. Best dressed my ass!"

Melvin leaned back and pointed his finger at Wendy. He was momentarily speechless. Yes, as he dug deep into his closet, his 1975 Earthshoes found their way onto his feet. And they weren't just any Earthshoes. They were clog Earthshoes at that.

"I'm gonna remember that, you just wait. And don't be tryin' to ride my jock later, either. You aint that fine anyway!"

Melvin walked over and snatched his cart from against the wall and headed for the elevator.

"Smells like split pea today Mel, mmm … mmm … good, mmm … mmm … good, that's how Melvin's pits smell, mmm … mmm … good!" Wendy sang out.

Melvin was steaming. Wendy usually gave him a hard time but he thought today would be different. He had no idea that she really didn't know about his good fortune, but he figured money wouldn't influence her anyway.

As he approached the elevator, he saw the office door of his new good friend, Mr. Carr. Melvin parked his cart in front of his office and stepped inside. He walked right past his secretary.

"Excuse me!" she called to Melvin.

"He's expectin' me."

Melvin stepped into the VP's office before she could stop him.

"What in the hell are you still doing here? You do know that you're out of a job, don't you?"

Melvin walked over to Mr. Carr's desk and leaned on it. Still pissed at Wendy, he looked at Mr. Carr and smiled. Mr. Carr looked back at Melvin with his usual smug, pompous glare. His secretary stepped into the office, but Mr. Carr quickly waved her back out.

"Well, what do you want?"

"I came to apologize, sir."

Feeling important, Mr. Carr leaned back in his big executive leather chair. He looked Melvin from head to toe then turned away so as to not look at him before he spoke.

"Is that so?"

Melvin walked around to Mr. Carr.

"Yes sir, I wanted to apologize and offer you a gift of forgiveness. Maybe you'll see just what kind of guy I really am and perhaps have a change of heart."

Mr. Carr spun his chair around and stared up at Melvin looking confused. Just then, Melvin slid his right hand down inside his gray sweatpants, into his crotch. He juggled his testicles for a second then retrieved his damp, musty hand from his two sweaty nut sacks. He leaned over and wiped his hand over Mr. Carr's face and neck while holding him down by the shoulder.

Melvin started laughing uncontrollably.

"What in the hell are you doing? SECURITY! Samantha, get security in here!" Mr. Carr yelled.

"I wanted to give you my forgiveness gift. So do you forgive me now?"

Melvin slammed his hand back down in his pants and quickly yanked it out. Mr. Carr attempted to get out of the seat, but Melvin held him down. While holding him firmly, Melvin took his sweat and pubic hair mix coated hand and began rubbing it through the petrified Mr. Carr's hair.

"You're crazy! Plain crazy I say! Security! Samantha, where is Security?"

Melvin walked to the door and looked back at Mr. Carr.

"If any of your friends want to know what that ravishin' new scent is that you're wearin', just tell them it's my new cologne. It's called RC5 or better known as Rotten Crotch No. 5. Tell them I also make women's perfume too, I call it The Sweat of My Balls! Sounds French, doesn't it? By the way, your wife loves it. Hey, you have a good day and your hair looks great! Is that mousse?"

Melvin headed out in a rush to avoid security again. Samantha, Mr. Carr's secretary rushed in after Melvin had left. Mr. Carr sat wiping his face with hand sanitizer while she kept inquiring about what had happened. Shortly after, two security guards entered Mr. Carr's office, but it was too late. Melvin was gone.

Melvin had just stepped into the elevator still laughing when it hit him. His stomach started gurgling and cramping. He pushed the button marked "G" on the elevator panel then backed into the corner and pushed the mail cart against the wall. Once the doors had closed, Melvin stood gritting his teeth and clenching his buttocks.

"I thought I was done with this shit. What could possibly be left in there? It must have been those tacos and the beer or maybe that damn egg salad and onion sandwich."

Melvin gripped onto the mail cart trying to keep this evil demon of misty bowel trapped inside its fleshy container. That's when he realized a very important fact.

"Hell, today's my last damn day," and without hesitation, Melvin leaned over the mail cart and blew out a blast of gas that would have frightened any creature, big or small. It resembled the stench of a thousand dead corpses. He then stood upright and shook the remaining stench out of his right pant leg. He rubbed his hand along the back of his leg and buttock just to ensure that a mass of air was the only thing that had escaped.

"Damn, that's just nasty. I thought after this mornin', my ass tank was on 'E'. Guess not. Boy, do I smell like some foul shit!"

Melvin reached over and banged on the "G" button a few more times, hoping to have a non-stop trip to his floor.

"6…5…" Melvin felt his knees buckle slightly as the elevator quickly slowed down, then stopped. "Ding!"

Melvin stepped back behind the cart and waited for the doors to open. When the doors opened, to his surprise, no one was there. Melvin smiled to himself, leaned forward and pushed the door close button at the bottom of the panel. The doors began to close slowly.

"Going down?" a voice yelled.

Melvin said nothing. He just stood quietly behind the cart with his eyes watering from the fetid stench that still lingered in the small, confined space.

Placing his briefcase between the doors, a neatly dressed gentleman forced the doors open and stepped in.

"Thanks," he said sarcastically.

Melvin just stood looking up at the numbers of the floors. The gentleman looked over at Melvin and then he too, became overly interested in the illumination of the little boxes above the elevator door.

"I know he smells this shit," Melvin was thinking.

The man started adjusting his tie and then started clearing his throat and coughing.

"That's right, take your time. Don't inhale too much, too fast. You gotta crawl before you can walk baby, 'cause this shit will kill ya."

Melvin watched the man squirm. The man looked over at Melvin again while sniffing.

"Yeah, I did it! It's mine! It's killin' you isn't it?" Melvin yelled out in his mind.

Another loud ding caught both men's attention. The box labeled "2" was illuminated. The elevator stopped and the doors opened. Standing in front of the door was a short dumpy woman. Melvin would have loved to watch a woman stand there and try to inhale the moldy cheese and hot garbage platter that he so distastefully prepared, but he couldn't. It was Joan, a woman that he knew. She was one of Wendy's girlfriends with whom she often went to lunch and since Melvin still desired Wendy, he didn't want to taint his image any more than it already was. Melvin pulled the bulky cart away from the wall and pushed it toward the door.

"Coming out, Hun."

He looked over at the gentleman and began shaking his head with a look of disgust on his face.

As he walked by Joan, he whispered, "Some people, man. Just triflin'!"

Melvin walked away looking back at the elevator still shaking his head. He could see the frown on their disgusted faces as the door closed. He walked around to the east corridor and caught the elevator down to the mailroom.

They both stood inside his office. Black bus driver hats, short black jackets with the big round red and white patches on the upper sleeve that read, "Westingate Security". Their uniforms also consisted of faded white shirts, with clip-on neckties that hung just above their navels. They even had on the tight, black polyester, above the ankle slacks, and the shiny, black, plastic covered shoes.

As Melvin entered his office, both men approached him. One was pointing his flashlight at him gesturing him to come quickly. Melvin walked right by both of the men; turning slightly as to avoid gut contact, because both men looked as if they had just finished eating a family reunion chicken pack from Popeye's. He reached over on his desk, grabbed a pen and a piece of paper and scribbled sloppily, "I QUIT," signed and dated it at the bottom. Just as he turned to leave, he could see a shadow growing larger with each nearing step. Melvin looked at one of the security officers.

"Man, I have a shirt just like that. Well, it's over at my buddy Dave's crib, but I do have one. Yep, it's got the same name plate holes and everything. What size you wear? I mean, I don't think that I'll need it anymore. You can have it if you need an extra."

Just then the voice from the large shadow yelled into the room. "That's him officers, arrest him!"

As the guards were turning back towards Melvin, he rushed between the two of them. He turned and positioned himself up on one leg with his arms extended like a bird. He was the "Karate Kid". He stood there with his leg shaking from trying to hold it up, his armpits stinking and holding gas.

"We can do this the easy way or the hard way gentlemen, your choice. You see this here stance? It's called the Crane. This here stance is guaranteed to bust yo ass. I learned this from a Chinese master up in Iowa, one of those small kick ass islands near China. So don't fuck around or I'll have to tax some ass!"

The guards stood there laughing. To see this overweight guy with two holes on the inside of the inner thighs of his sweatpants and trying to hold his thick flabby leg up was hilarious.

"Well don't just stand there, do something. Arrest him," Mr. Carr yelled.

The security guards did nothing. They pointed to Melvin's resignation and let him go. Melvin walked up to Mr. Carr and jumped at him making him flinch. He then let out a blast of gas from hell and slowly walked off. The three men stood at the front door fanning the foul odor as they watched Melvin limp to his car.

CHAPTER 6   THE CELEBRATION

The lights were dim and the sounds of Frankie Beverly and Maze filled the entire building and beyond. Everybody was dancing, drinking, and having a good time on Melvin's dime.

Melvin and Dave sat at the end of the bar drinking and trying to work their magic on two women who had come in with a friend of Dave's. They appeared to be pretty stuck on themselves. Overdressed and really not that attractive, they were a step up from the usual regular women that passed through The Sapphire. Melvin complimented the women on their superior cleavage displaying techniques, and the fullness of their buxom bottoms. They just turned up their noses and continued their boring intellectual conversation on the cultural effects of today's entrepreneur and free enterprise. All they talked about was making money. Of course, this bored Melvin to no end.

He soon blocked out their boring debate and sat quietly for awhile, thinking only about leaving the mailroom, the money, Uncle Cleve and the house and car that he had left him, Wendy, and the little lady who tried to enlighten his game.

Both ladies were looking at Melvin as he sat in his daze wondering what type of woman he'd like and more so, how much he'd be willing to spend on one. They both smelled money as easily as money hounds do. They looked at Melvin and saw nothing but huge dollars signs. They were both being cautious, making sure that neither blocked the other of their chance. One of the ladies looked over at the other and to let her know that she was about to make her move. She inched closer to Melvin then started in on him.

"So how does it feel to be rich Mel? Huh, how does it feel?" she repeated as she leaned closer pressing her breast slightly against the bar.

Melvin looked down at her breast, then up to her eyes realizing that this young lady had class and was not like the usual swamp dog that he was accustomed to dragging into his or any other bed. He decided to think before answering for a change. Using the little old lady's advice, he decided to use a different tactic. He leaned over and whispered softly in her ear.

"Look here baby; I'm no different than I was a few days ago. As a matter of fact, I'm on your set baby. Hell, you write the script, I just read the lines, it's all about bein' in your world."

She stood up and wrapped both her arms around Melvin's neck and kissed him on the cheek.

"That was deep Melvin, wow! I had no idea you were so, so... ah screw it, you wanna fuck?"

Mel leaned back in shock thinking to himself, "You mean that bullshit actually works? Damn, I guess sluts come in all classes."

That's when he noticed her shoes. She had on a nice stylish outfit, but her shoes were old with the heels worn on each side which made her stand as if she were bow legged. Even Melvin knew that was a no-no. Melvin quickly brushed that fashion defect from his mind and decided to go for it.

Melvin leaned over to whisper into the young lady's ear, but without realizing that he was actually yelling in order to be heard over the loud music.

"Look here Baby, what you like, albums or CDs?"

The young woman smiled at Melvin and without hesitation yelled back, "CDs!"

"Well don't go too far 'cause I'm plannin' on lettin' you 'CDs' nuts all night!"

"Promise?"

"Oh you know that's right."

Melvin looked over to Dave, who was humming the lyrics to 'Joy and Pain' as it played throughout the room. "You enjoyin' yourself man?"

Dave raised his glass which was filled with his favorite brand of rum with just a splash of coke, "Hell yeah! I'm havin' a good time."

Melvin looked at both of the ladies sitting beside them and then back at Dave, and yelled back at him.

"Which one of these hos you want tonight? They're game and I'm payin'. You can have your choice between two middle class, intellectual, private school, world renowned, high society perpetratin' sluts."

With his mouth wide open, Dave slowly lowered his glass. Both women jumped out of their seats, cursing Melvin while grabbing their jackets.

"You don't have THAT much money, you fat fuck! You'll never get any of this. You're not even in the same league as us," one shouted as they rushed out of The Sapphire.

"Yeah, well I've got enough money to replace those run over heels on those raggedy ass shoes. You damn gold diggas!" Melvin shouted at the now closed door.

Everyone in the club was now looking at Melvin. The DJ had cut the sound and removed his headphones from his ears. Melvin and Dave looked at each other. Melvin took a sip from his glass and looked back at the door.

"I guess they weren't hos after all," Melvin said while starting to laugh.

"Fool, you're crazy!" Dave yelled out, and everyone began to laugh. He slumped over the bar laughing hysterically.

"Did you see that bitch's face?"

"Yeah, she looked like she was ready to rip your balls off."

"Only for a price, damn gold digger. She needed to roll out with her fake ass and all that fake hair. The ho had just offered me some pussy then got all uptight 'cause I called her out.

You know I can't deal with those fake hussies. If you're a ho, be a ho. I mean, take pride in what you're good at."

Dave stopped laughing and looked at Mel seriously.

"But the ho did have some nice tits, damn!"

Both men resumed laughing, touched glasses and went back to drinking and talking.

Later that night, both men sat at the bar half drunk, watching the ladies in the electric slide line and trying to make a selection.

"Damn, why is it that every woman who can't get a dance the whole damn night, jumps up and runs her ass on the dance floor as soon as the first note to `Electric Slide` is played? What? You can't get up and dance by yourself to any other song? Look at em', just pitiful," Melvin slurred.

"Man, just pick!"

"Man, I'm gettin' tired of these ugly ass women, Dave. Either they're ugly, jobless, or just way too big for me man, but I think it's gonna be the big, ugly, jobless sweaty one over there, third row on the left, with the ass big enough to sit my drink on. Do you know her? I've never seen her in here before. I would have remembered that ass. An ass like that, you just roll her over and salute it first, and you know you gotta slap that thing! Oh yeah, she looks broke enough to go out with me. Damn, with that ass, she reminds me of an ostrich. Man, I might have to ride her ass up outta here."

Both men started their contagious laughter once again, downed their drinks and then made their way over to the ladies.

Dave and Melvin jumped in the group of ladies and joined in the uniform line dance. Melvin was dancing wildly while singing with the music.

"Are you comin' with me... let me take you on a party ride... you got to move, move... "

He inched his way over until he was behind the protruding round fleshed woman. He began to sing even louder as he waved his arms in the air until he got her attention. She looked over and smiled at him. That was all he needed.

As the line made its shift, Melvin slid in behind the woman and was now holding her close as he continued to sing. She welcomed his embrace and began to sing along with him. Dave was by the wall talking to a young lady that he had his eye on for most of the night. She too, was in the line, but instead of acting as ridiculous as Melvin, he decided to pull her over to the side and dance with her.

After a few songs had ended, Dave headed back to the bar with his new found date. They began to drink and laugh. Soon after, Melvin returned to the bar with not the lady he had intended, but a small built woman who looked as if she had come to The Sapphire straight from church.

Her hair was pulled back in what I like to refer to as a "librarian bun". She had on thick bifocals with thick plastic frames. Her dress was plain and hung just above her ankles and she had on flat heeled shoes. To say the least, Dave saw no sex appeal in her. Dave rose from his stool, and Melvin introduced them.

"Dave this here is uh, uh…"

"Cheryl, nice to meet you." She interrupted while extending her hand towards Dave.

"Likewise. You havin' a good time?"

"Yeah, your buddy is so crazy. He's somethin' else."

She turned and walked over to the young lady that Dave had brought over to the table and gently placed her hand on her shoulder.

Dave grabbed Melvin by the arm and pulled him over to the side of the bar. He started gesturing with both hands as he pointed the palms of his hands to the heavens.

"What happened to 'Super Ass'? When I looked over, you were all over that. What happened?"

"Man, I had to let that slide."

"For that? For, Ms. I-Don't-Screw? She looks like a fuck-in' librarian for cryin' out loud."

"Nah man, we just happened. She just rolled up and I went with it. The ostrich chick reminded me of 'Betty Crocker' so I had to back off."

"Betty Crocker? What's Betty Crocker got to do with her? Wait, let me guess. You're now gonna tell me that her teeth were so yella that it reminded you of cake icin' right? No, you're gonna go on and on about how she was sweatin' like she had just stepped out of an oven. I know it's somethin' dumb. Too dumb to give up that nice ass though, I'm sure. I've got it, you're gonna stand here and tell me that the woman in all her ass splendor, smelled like cake which made you hungry, right?"

"Nope, she smelled like ass!"

"Well what in the hell has that got to do with Betty Crock-er?"

"You know Betty's ass had to stink, all that time workin' in that hot ass kitchen. That's what she smelled like, sweaty ass and hot muffins, made me nauseous, too. How you think that made me feel? I was ridin' that big wad of flesh. The entire time, I was hungry, horny, and heavin'. "

"Man you've got issues, serious issues. So you're gonna waste your night with this slug huh?"

"No, I know she's not tryin' to do nothin'. I just wanted the other ladies to see me with her so they'd talk about how much better I could do by bein' with them."

"Smart thinkin' man. Ok, let's go over and talk to them for awhile then you can get rid of the book worm and grab a fresh one. Make it short, 'cause I'm already ready to get my freak on."

The men walked back over to their new acquaintances. The two ladies were old friends from high school. By the time the guys had gotten back over to them, they were heavily en-grossed in conversation and laughter.

"So what are you ladies talkin' about over here?" Melvin asked grinning.

The librarian looking young lady turned to Melvin and smiled. "I was suggesting that we take you two handsome guys somewhere and screw your brains out, but Sheila doesn't want to look like a slut."

Both women started laughing. Melvin and Dave looked at each other in shock. Dave's mouth was sitting wide open as he walked towards his date.

"That wouldn't make you a slut baby. I'm just flattered that you find me that attractive."

He winked at Melvin. Melvin turned and waved to the bartender. He pulled out a rolled up stack of money and laid twelve one hundred dollar bills on the bar.

"This is my tab limit. Tell these clowns that they can pay for their own drinks after this runs out."

The bartender acknowledged Melvin and the men waved to the crowd as they escorted the women through The Sapphire and out the door.

Once outside, Melvin opened the door for Cheryl and they both climbed in the back seat. Dave walked around to the driver's side of the car and left his date to fend for herself. She opened the door to the passenger side and climbed in. Melvin, not quite as drunk as he wanted to be, reached down on the floor and picked up the bag that he and Dave had stashed there prior to entering The Sapphire. It contained more beer, a pint of vodka, rum, and a bottle of Coca Cola. He opened up the bag and pulled out the small stack of tiny paper cups. He filled one of the cups about a quarter of the way full with some of the rum and then grabbed the bottle of coke.

"Who wants a drink?"

Sheila turned and looked at Melvin and held out her hand. She was already pretty buzzed.

"I'll have one. You want one Baby?" she asked Dave.

"I'm cool Baby."

Dave was now focused on nothing else but getting her to a hotel to have his way with her. Melvin completed the mixture by adding a little of the coke and passed it to Sheila.

"Girl, you look like you've had enough already."

"I'm feeling good. So where are we going? Let's party. I've never hung out with no high rollers before."

She downed the drink and extended her cup for a refill. Melvin repeated the mix and passed the cup back once again. After filling another cup with the same liquid mix, he offered the cup to Cheryl.

"Oh I'm cool. I'm not much of a drinker, but I did have two in The Sapphire."

Melvin downed the drink and then another. He kept pouring and he and Sheila kept drinking. Melvin was now feeling pretty buzzed. He leaned over and started kissing Cheryl's neck and grabbing at her breast. She kissed him back but removed his hand from her breast. Melvin leaned back and placed her hand between his legs.

"You like that? Come on and do somethin' with it."

Cheryl began to blush. She turned her head away and giggled.

"Not now, maybe later."

"Maybe later, what do you mean, maybe? C'mon girl quit playin'. Let me see what you got."

With this, Sheila clumsily made her way to her knees and leaned over the back of the seat to watch. Melvin was now leaning back in the seat with his hips pushed up as he unzipped his pants. He unsnapped the button on his trousers and started to pull them down towards his knees. Cheryl placed her hand on Melvin's arm and leaned over. She tried to speak low enough for his ears to hear only.

"I don't do that Melvin."

"You don't do what?"

"That. I don't do blowjobs."

"What? Stop playin', come on and hit this girl."

"Seriously, I don't do that."

Dave looked in the rearview mirror shaking his head for Melvin to see. He then looked over at his heavily intoxicated date and asked the same question of her.

"How 'bout you sweet thing, you get down with that or what?"

"Hell ye......."

Melvin screamed out, "You drunk ass stank ho, aww hell no!"

"Screeeeeeeeeeeeetch!" The car came to an abrupt stop. Dave jumped out and opened the back door then walked around and opened the passenger side door and pulled Sheila out of the car. Cheryl walked over and helped her on the curb and bent her over while patting her back. Just as Sheila was about to answer Dave's question, she vomited right over the seat onto Melvin. Dave knew that she was done for the night and no fun would come out of nursing a sick woman all night.

Melvin climbed out and began brushing off his pants. He closed the door and climbed in the passenger seat.

"Y'all just gone leave us out here?" Cheryl yelled out.

"Damn right! Take her drunk ass home." Melvin yelled back then threw a fifty dollar bill out of the window. Dave was pissed. They drove to the nearest gasoline station to clean the inside of the car. After the car was wiped down, Dave walked up to the thick fiber glass window and bought two evergreen scented tree car fresheners. He slid back in the driver's side to an awaiting Melvin. Still brushing off his pants, he reached up and grabbed one of the scented trees and started briskly rubbing it up and down his pant leg. Dave placed the key into the ignition.

"Where to, man? What you want to do now?"

Melvin looked back at the back seat then over at Dave.

"Do you see any pussy back there? I mean, that is the objective for the night, isn't it?"

"Yeah, but I just figured since the incident with the car and all."

"Man turn this car around and head back to The Sapphire before all the women leave."

Dave put the car in gear and off they went. They sped back towards the club. As they drove, they saw Cheryl and Sheila sitting in the weather shelter of the bus stop. Cheryl tried flagging Dave down, but they continued on.

They pulled back into The Sapphire parking lot and hurried back inside. The party was still jumping. Both men walked over to the bar and Melvin waved the bartender over.

"What's my tab lookin' like?"

The bartender walked over to the cash register and picked up the wide white thin cardboard receipt. He slid it back under the register and walked back over to Melvin.

"Seven twenty eight."

"Damn, these are some drinkin' motha fuckas! Ok, hook us up with two rum and cokes and tell DJ Steve to kick that 'Electric Slide' joint again."

The bartender acknowledged him and walked off. After getting their drinks, Melvin and Dave sat at the bar. They knew that the women selecting song was soon to start. DJ Steve played the song and up jumped the women who had been matted to their seats.

"Ok, ok, pick fast. We gotta get out of here just in case the other two come back."

The men downed their drinks and rushed over to the dance floor. Before the song was over both men had gotten two women to join them at the bar. It was much easier this time. Most of the women there were pretty drunk due to Melvin's generosity of the "open bar". The men wasted no time making sexual advancements toward the women. Once they agreed to accompany the men, they left.

They rushed the women out of the club. They all climbed into the car and pulled off. After riding for over fifteen minutes, Dave couldn't hold it. He had to ask.

"Damn girl, you've got some nice lips. I bet you could work those pretty lips of yours, too."

The woman looked over at Dave and responded.

"Damn right! You can find out right now if you think you can handle it."

Dave smiled. The woman leaned over and unzipped him and began to do what he was in need of all night. The car's speed dropped from forty miles per hour to about ten. Dave was driving like a ninety year old man as the woman went to work.

Melvin leaned back and started tugging at his zipper while smiling at his date.

She smiled back at Melvin.

"I don't do that. I'll fuck, but I don't suck. Sorry. Hey does anybody smell vomit?"

Melvin sat up and began tapping on the back of Dave's seat.

"Dave. Dave. I say Dave!"

Dave couldn't hear him. He was in his own world. Melvin leaned back in the seat. Realizing that he was stuck with this woman for the rest of the night he leaned over and kissed her. They talked and fondled each other. She was willing to do just about anything except dampen his organ. After Dave was satisfied, the car sped up. He noticed a liquor store on the opposite side of the street. He made a "U" turn and pulled into the parking lot. He walked in and returned with more rum, coke and cups. They mixed up a few drinks and sat talking and drinking for a while then headed for the hotel.

CHAPTER 7   THE MORNING AFTER

The blade of the axe was just at the tip of his skull. Well at least that's how it felt. Melvin's head was pounding like crazy. His eyes felt like someone had stuck pins through both of them. His teeth were hurting, the tips of his fingers were aching, and he had a burning sensation in his upper groin area.

Through one eye he looked around the room and had noticed his pants lying on the floor and one of his shoes was lodged between a writing table and a couch. His shirt was balled up in the corner and his belt was draped over the air conditioning unit. As he opened his other eye, he felt the burning intensify in his crotch. He pulled the cover from over his left thigh as he began to sit up in the bed. Melvin looked down at his crotch area, and grunted, "What the…?"

He looked up at the ceiling trying to think of how in the world he had gotten a bald spot in his pubic hair. He continued looking around the room for his other shoe and his jacket when he noticed a skirt and a woman's blouse folded neatly on the ottoman that was placed next to the beige wing back chair. A woman's jacket was hanging from the top corner of the chair and a pair of high heel shoes was lying on top of the neatly folded clothes.

As Melvin sat dabbing at his wound, he felt movement next to him. The covers slid off his legs as the figure turned in the opposite direction. Melvin reached for the top of the covers, and slowly pulled them back producing a large dark image. As Melvin leaned toward the figure, the head turned and she spoke those two deadly words,

"Good Morning!"

Melvin retreated. He sat and thought for a second and realized that he had to ask. Not remembering her name or how they got there, Melvin decided he'd casually ask a few questions before shooting off at the mouth. He thought he'd better use a little tact.

"Excuse me, Baby." Melvin now started tapping her shoulder.

"Hey, Melvin baby, good morning."

Melvin stood up, baring his naked bottom. He walked over and picked his pants up off the floor, then walked over and slid his underwear off the top of the television. After tussling with his underwear and trousers, Melvin went and sat down on the bed. He placed his head in his hand and grunted some more.

"Look here Baby; I've got four questions for you. One, who in the hell are you? 'B', how in the hell did we get here? Three, what's with the bald spot, and 'A', who in the HELL shit in your mouth, 'cause your breath smells like all to be damned?!"

The woman sat up rubbing her hands through her hair, and pulling the covers over her bare chest. Trying to conceal her hurt and embarrassment, she looked away from Melvin and spoke to him in a very low voice.

"Well I guess everything you said to me last night was just bullshit. My name is Lisa, remember? We met last night at The Sapphire. You said that I was everything that you ever needed in a woman, and now that you were well off, you wanted a down to earth, around the way girl, who was real, to be with you."

Melvin sat and grunted while rubbing his temple. The woman slid back down into the bed, now speaking with a cracking voice.

"I told you that I didn't usually do this, but you seemed so nice. Oh yeah, and sorry about the bald spot. I guess that's my fault, too."

Melvin lifted his head, and turned slightly toward the woman. She rolled over on her stomach and placed her face in her hands and started to cry.

"How did it happen? Did you bite me or what?"

The woman stopped crying just long enough to explain.

"You kept pushing my head down there, and I told you to stop but you wouldn't. I told you that I didn't do that, but you were so drunk and kept on insisting. Then you grabbed my head and rubbed my face in your crotch. When you pulled my head up, my braces had gotten caught in your hair. You yanked back so fast; I don't think you knew what had happened. Hey, where's my girlfriend?"

Lisa started crying again. Melvin slid closer to her.

"Morning breath, you have heard of it haven't you, especially after a night of drinkin'? Surely you don't think that your breath smells like roses. You could stand to be sucking on a mint or two, yourself," she whined out. "Damn Melvin, all the nice things that you said to me to get me here. Did you mean any of it?"

Now wiping her eyes, Lisa rolled back over and sat up against the headboard of the bed. Melvin slid even closer. As he looked at Lisa, he realized that she really was an attractive girl. She had a sensitive look to her, fragile even. She looked so different than she did last night. Rum has a way of doing that. Melvin took his hand and placed it on the side of her face to wipe away a tear. He looked her in the eyes and spoke to her calmly.

"Bullshit baby, it's all bullshit. You need to be gettin' dressed so we can roll 'cause I got shit to do."

Melvin walked over to the window and saw his Escort sitting in the hotel parking lot so he knew Dave was around somewhere. He pulled his cell phone out of his jacket pocket and called Dave.

"What man?" Dave answered.

"Let's go Shorty; we gotta go check out the spot today."

Melvin flipped his phone shut and gathered up the rest of his clothing. He got dressed. Lisa was taking her time putting on her clothes. After she had slipped on her shoes, she and Melvin walked down to the car without saying a word to each other. Dave and his date made their way downstairs about fifteen minutes later. They all piled in the car and drove back to The Sapphire where the women had parked their cars the night before. At The Sapphire they let the ladies out of the car.

"Hope to see you again Melvin. I had a wonderful time."

Melvin said nothing. He didn't even get out and walk Lisa to her car. While Dave walked his date to the car, Melvin climbed into the driver's seat. After Dave had returned, Melvin started the car and sped off. He dropped Dave off, and then headed home.

"I'll be back in about a half hour," Melvin yelled out to Dave through the car window. Dave threw up his hand as he headed up the stairs to the entrance of his building.

Melvin got home and jumped in the shower. While applying the soap to his alcohol saturated, overly sexed body, he could feel the stinging sensation of his scalped pubic area. He got out of the shower, brushed his teeth, and took a quick shave. He reached up in his medicine cabinet and pulled down the dark bottle of peroxide. He ripped off a small piece of toilet paper from the roll and drenched it with the liquid. He dabbed it onto the bald hair ripped spot. The bruise foamed up like the head of a poorly poured glass of beer. Melvin replaced the top on the peroxide bottle and placed it back in the cabinet. He reached for the jar of "Blue Star Ointment" and removed the top. Jabbing his finger in the jar, Melvin pulled a glob of the gel out and slapped it on his wound.

"Oh shit!" he yelled out, as the ointment burned its way over the bald area. Melvin eased his underwear on and walked out of the bathroom dragging his left leg behind him as if he had been shot there.

Melvin returned to his bedroom, popped the top to his laundry basket open, and retrieved a pair of jeans. He grabbed a shirt from his closet, slipped on his socks and shoes, and headed back out the door.

Once in the car, Melvin called Dave from his cell phone to let him know that he was on his way. When Melvin approached Dave's building, he could see Dave walking down the sidewalk talking and making exchanges with most of the people that he passed. Dave climbed in the car. "Damn, didn't I just leave your ass?"

Melvin looked over at Dave as if he wanted to say something smart back, but he couldn't. Dave had been his friend for so long and had gotten Melvin out of so many jams. He would get him high for free, and would turn him on to free sex occasionally.

"Look here man, let's go check out the place, I'm sure it's a nice size, and..." Melvin paused. "You know, if you ever want to leave this area and hang out on my new end, you're more than welcome man, and maybe you can stop sellin' that shit, too."

Dave sat up and placed both his hands in his jacket pockets. He started biting on his bottom lip. He stared out the windshield of the car.

"Leave my place? Man, I aint never leavin' my spot. I like it there, and that shit I sell, hell, it's paid for your car to get fixed when you aint have the bread. It even paid your rent on occasion. So what? You gettin' all high and mighty already?"

Dave didn't look at Melvin, and Mel could tell that he had pissed him off.

"Look man, I'm just sayin', we boys right? We've always been there for each other. I just want to make sure that you know that I got your back."

Dave looked at Melvin, who continued to watch the road.

"If you've got my back so much, why haven't we stopped to get somethin' to eat? I'm hungry as hell. You know pleasin' women the way I do makes a brotha hungry."

Both men started laughing. It was their way of letting each other know that things were cool.

"Can I take your order?" the cashier at the Burger King asked. Both men ordered their food. Melvin unzipped his jacket to pull his wallet out of the inside pocket.

"Wait, oh hell no!" Dave yelled.

He burst into laughter, and then walked away yelling, "We gotta talk man, WE HAVE GOT TO TALK!"

Melvin walked over to the booth where Dave was sitting still snickering to himself. Melvin sat down and pushed the tray to the center of the table.

"What?" Mel asked with a strange look on his face. Dave started laughing again. Melvin, looking frustrated, yelled out again, "WHAT?"

Dave started waving his hand and shaking his head to signal Mel to wait. After he had calmed down, Dave took a sip from his cup of Coke. Melvin leaned forward and started to remove his jacket, and out shot the Coke. Dave had spit out all of the liquid from his mouth and started laughing uncontrollably.

"Man, if you don't tell me what in the hell is so funny, I'm gonna choke the shit out of you right now," Melvin yelled while reaching for his friends throat.

After collecting himself, Dave took a deep breath. He looked at Melvin then looked outside through the big glass window.

"Bro, how you gonna come out here with a Hawaiian shirt on man? Who in the hell do you think you are? Don Ho?"

Dave started laughing once again, but Melvin failed to see the humor in it. "I'm about as much in the Ho family as your momma! As a matter of fact, I saw her at the last Ho reunion."

Melvin started laughing and pointing at Dave. Dave didn't take offense to the crack about his mother. His mother was like a mother to Melvin, too. Melvin loved her as if she was his own mom. It was all in fun.

Melvin continued, "You talkin'? Man before you got rolled up in cash, boy I remember back in the day and you were no damn Denzel yourself. Hell, you were a 'Ready For The World' curl activated, tummy tie shirt sportin', nut crushin' biker shorts wearin', wanna be Michael Jackson clown. How you gonna talk about anybody's gear Thriller boy? You still got your glove?"

Dave started laughing then chucked a couple of fries in his mouth. He swallowed the food and started in on Melvin.

"Oh no, boy, back in the day you were a swollen, snaggled toothed, nappy dread havin', flip flop flippin', too tight Bermuda short wearin', gas passin' bastard. Hell, you aint changed at all! Those snags still look like they could rip open a can or two."

They sat there for over an hour going back and forth on one another. Then they finally walked over to the soda bar and refilled their cups before leaving. They got in the car, and pulled out of the parking lot and headed for the Woodrow Wilson Bridge for his future home site, Mount Vernon.

CHAPTER 8   THE PLANTATION

The bricks stood out from all the other homes on the block. The black and red historic look, presented a classy appearance. The wrought iron fence, which surrounded the perimeter, was separated every eight feet by pillars of the same matching brick. A solid block of concrete one square foot and three inches in height topped each pillar.

The wrought iron gate was black with a stylish design of black roses streaming between each rod. The gate was open on both sides, resting on the brownish colored grass and matted leaves. The concrete driveway produced a subtle incline deep into the yard with weeping willow trees lining the path. It ran beyond the trees and in front of the house, into a large semi-circle, which branched off into the four-car garage. The house itself wasn't huge, but extremely impressive. It had a large front porch with six white columns around it. White pickets and railings filled the space of each column, and beautiful hard wood flooring ran from each end. Even the shutters on the windows were pure white, as if they had just been painted.

In front of the house sat a 1972 gold Chevy Impala.

"Damn, he was still drivin' that shit? He had this same car ever since I can remember. Yo man, you want it?"

"Nope! I aint drivin' that piece of shit," Dave mumbled with a straight face.

"Well you know I'll be replacing that piece of crap with somethin' fly. I can't be seen in that. You know I'll have to sport a Benz or maybe a Bema. You want the Escort?"

"Nope, I aint drivin' this piece of shit either, if you get some new fly shit, I'll be drivin' your new fly shit, too! I'm sure that my ass can fit in the same seat that your ass has sat in. It'll be like sittin' my ass in a wash tub after you've spread the seat out, but hey!"

"Yeah, whateva!"

They continued looking around the front yard.

"Man, I didn't know Unk was rollin' like this. Damn, this shit is tight! It looks like one of those southern plantation joints, doesn't it? This is some George Washington, Kunta Kinte type shit here! Can you believe this Dee? It's all mine. Whoa!"

Melvin stepped out of the car and walked over to the stone birdbath and fountain set in the grass just off of the driveway. Mounted on top of the bath was a statue of a little boy urinating into the bowl.

"Oh, you know this shit's gotta go. There's no way I'm gonna have some little white boy out here pissin' in a bowl that poor little birds will be drinkin' from and bathin' in. It's bad enough that some poor bird will have to drink from the same water that another bird had just dunked his balls in. And you know me, hell, I might come home drunk one night, all dehydrated and shit, and I'll wind up havin' my damn lips perched right up against his little dick sippin' my ass off! How's that gone look, man? What'll the neighbors say, huh?"

Dave got out and placed his hand on the roof of the car.

"You know, you're just nasty enough to do that shit too, but I'll tell you what, if you're thirsty right now, I've got a stream that I've been storin' up ever since we left Burger King. It's probably not as cold as his, but I'd be more than happy to give you a few sips. I don't know, you look more like a gulper though. The straw's a bit thick, but it has a fat bubble tip for you to rest your lips on while you're sippin'! The juice may be a little tart too, but if you sip on it long enough it'll turn into a warm shake!"

Dave burst out laughing even harder, slapping his hand on the roof of the car.

"That's some nasty shit man, and some nasty gay shit at that!" Melvin yelled out while laughing uncontrollably.

"Hey, just consider it practice for the little stone boy, and don't worry, I can make this straw stone hard, too!" Dave screamed out while tugging on the zipper on his pants almost in tears.

The men enjoyed a good laugh from that and continued laughing as they walked up the steps to the large double doors.

Melvin dug into his jacket pocket and pulled out the key ring that Mr. Kohl had given him. After trying several keys, he slid the tarnished key that was largest on the ring into the keyhole and turned it. He pushed open the door, and that's when they heard the squealing sound from across the fence.

"Hello, yoohoo, boys, heeeeeeeellooo."

Dave and Mel looked over at the fence and then back at each other.

The voice yelled out once more, "Boys, over here, hello, heeeeeello!"

Melvin tapped Dave on the arm and gestured with his head for him to walk over to the fence with him.

As they neared the fence, they could see standing on the other side, between the hedges of the next yard, a lady signaling them over.

She was a small built woman, with skeleton like features. You could see every bone of her body protruding from her clothing. Her dirty gray hair hung down to her shoulders. It was thin, dull and lifeless. Her skin was pasty in color and ashy look-ing. Her eyes were sunken into her face and had dark shadows beneath the sockets; and painted over her thin cracked lips was the deepest apple red lipstick. Her clothes draped over her ano-rexic looking body as if she were a stick figure. With her pink pants rising above her ankles, no socks, and a pair of those, dirty white, plain, pointed toe, tie up, rubber bottom sneakers, she was truly a sight. Grabbing the side of her knitted sweater, she pulled it over her vacant breast area as if she was covering herself up. She placed her other hand on the pearl necklace that lay loosely around her neck and tucked them neatly under her collarless blouse.

Tightly holding her long thin cigarette wedged between her middle and index fingers of her right hand, she raised it up and pointed it at the boys while squinting her eyes to avoid the smoke.

"You boys here to cut the grass? Mr. Carlos doesn't do it anymore. Says nobody will pay him. You here to mow the lawn, or are you here to paint? If so, do you know the new people moving in?"

Once more, both men looked at each other, puzzled. Just as Melvin was about to speak, the small woman continued.

"You know the owner died? So you probably won't get paid if you cut it." She moved closer to the bars and took a drag from now red tipped stick.

Dave looked at Melvin. He placed his hands over his mouth then whispered low enough so that the small woman would not hear.

"Damn, if you've ever wanted to know what walkin' diphtheria looked like, there it is, in the flesh. That truly is a walkin' pile of shit. Sorry man, don't mean to talk about your new neighbor and all, but DAMN! This chick is scary. She reminds me of the Crypt Keeper on that HBO show. What's it called? Oh yeah, 'Tales From The Crypt'."

The woman continued telling the men about all the work that still required completion around the old house. After listening to all that he could stand, Melvin stepped up to the fence. He jingled the keys in his hand as he advanced then stopped at the fence and stood with his chest stuck out. He placed his hands in his jacket pockets and with a proud tone spoke to the woman.

"No we're not here to cut the grass or paint. I'm the new owner and your new neighbor, Melvin. That's why we're here today. My consultant and I came out to assess the necessary repairs. I'll probably have a crew out here sometime next week to get started."

The lady lowered her cigarette. Still continuing to squint her eyes, she looked Melvin up and down and then over at Dave. She mumbled just loud enough for the guys to hear.

"Oh, well I'll be, so where you boys from? So, were you a relative of Mr. Salter's? Are you planning on living here?"

The lady asked question after question. She then dropped her cigarette and mashed it into the ground with her shoe until the fire vanished.

"Yes, as a matter of fact, Mr. Salter was my uncle."

While watching her create the small indentation into the earth with her shoe, Melvin continued. "I'm not sure if I'm goin' to stay out here. Why do you ask?"

She looked at Melvin and smiled. She let go of her sweater and placed her hands on two of the bars of the fence. She then motioned the boys closer. She looked back toward the upper windows of her home and then down the side of the hedges. She motioned Melvin even closer, to within whispering range. Dave walked over and placed his hand on one of the bars and leaned in curiously. She placed her hand on Melvin's right arm and pressed her face between two of the bars. Melvin placed his ear next to her mouth and Dave got closer to hear what was so secretive. She began to whisper.

"I'm Marie. I was sorry to hear about your uncle. He was a nice man."

Melvin started to speak, but was cut off.

"He always took care of me, too. He loved me. Yep, your uncle really loved me. We've been through a lot, your uncle and I. I loved him, too, I guess. If it wasn't for that old bastard in there, we would have been together. Yep, your uncle was a really good lover, too. Are you a good lover? Are you going to take care of me like your uncle did? You do know what I mean don't you?"

Melvin shook his head from side to side demonstrating a negative response. Suddenly she spoke louder.

"You know, I hardly ever wear any panties! I'm not wearing any now and I love to fuck. Will you fuck me? Will you?"

Melvin turned and looked at her. He wasn't sure if he was hearing her right. She was now staring at Melvin with her eyes wide open and licking her lips. Just as he tried to speak again, Marie thrust out her tongue and licked Melvin up the side of his face.

"Oh shit! What in the hell are you doin'?" Melvin yelled out.

"Shhhhhhhh, he might hear us." She looked back at her house and down the side of the hedges again. "Don't worry, there's plenty more where that came from Baby. Anybody ever tell you that you look like Sydney Portier? I just love Sydney Portier."

Marie, now standing there gyrating, and jabbing her tongue back and forth, was stroking one of the bars with her right hand as if it were a penis. She began blowing kisses at Melvin, which forced the men to retreat.

"If there's more where that came from, then somebody needs to go back and burn that damn place down!" Melvin kept shouting at Marie while wiping his face.

Dave looked back at the woman who was now rubbing her crotch with her hand, and poking her tongue on the side of her cheek as if she were giving oral sex.

"Damn, that's just nasty. You should just shoot some shit like that. Let me put her crazy ass out of her misery!" Dave stood there pointing his finger at her as if it were a revolver. "C'mon, let me shoot her. I'll load my gun with some penicillin and peroxide bullets. I bet the bitch has the clap. Shhhhhhhhh! See, I told you, I can hear that nasty snatch drippin' from here. And you might wanna get checked for cooties, rabies, STD's or somethin', damn! Was it me, or did the old tramp's breath smell like she'd just had a shit sandwich and warm glass of piss for lunch? No sugar, no cream, just straight up piss."

Melvin walked over to the birdbath and started splashing his face with the water that ran from the little stone boy's penis.

"That old ho is crazy, and you're right, the ho's breath did smell like zoo dirt!"

Dave placed his hand over his face to hide his chuckling.

"You think your uncle really banged that nasty bitch? Damn, she's so old I bet that kitty cat probably can't even meow anymore."

Melvin looked at Dave then continued wiping his face with the sleeve of his jacket.

"No way, man. Nah, Uncle Cleve didn't commit suicide. Now if he had done that, then I might have believed her, 'cause you'd definitely have to kill yourself after tappin' some shit like that! And love that? No way. Not Unk!"

The guys headed back to the house still hearing the loud whisper from the fence.

"Call me! You're going to call me right? Hey neighbor! Can you hear me? Call me, Melvin. Okay? Let's get together before he knows that you live there. He's so jealous."

Dave looked back at her one last time then over at Melvin. Before he could get his words out, he began to laugh.

"Maybe your uncle hooked up with her from an electric slide line. She damn sure fits the profile."

Melvin didn't respond to Dave's attempt at humor. He was still upset with Marie for licking him. He looked back at her, and then wiped his face once more with his sleeve. He pulled the group of keys from his jacket pocket and unlocked the door once more. He slowly pushed the door open and they stepped in.

The inside of the house was dim and had a damp, musty smell. The furniture was covered with white sheets, and all of the curtains were drawn. The hardwood floors had no shine, and the large grandfather clock by the staircase had stopped working. There was electricity and heat, as the utility company had not yet turned them off, but no water.

Melvin walked over to a large object, which sat alone in the corner of the room. He removed the sheet, which had been draped over top and pulled the small chain, which hung from the side opening of the pole. In an instant, the room was illuminated.

Now seeing the room even better, they noticed just how nice it really was.

"You know I gotta drop a flat screen right here," Melvin motioned towards the wall over the fireplace.

"I'm pulling out all this old colonial bullshit furniture, and I'm gone hook this joint up!"

The men went though the entire house. They checked out every room, and Melvin described all the changes that he was going to make. After looking at the fourth bathroom, both men noticed something very odd. There was one room at the end of the hall that appeared very bright. This particular room produced a weird type of light, almost as if it glowed.

"What in the hell is that?"

Dave reached over and switched the hall light on. The room still looked lit up and appeared to be glowing. The men approached the room slowly. Melvin slid his arm against the half opened door and pushed it completely open. They stepped into the room and looked around.

"What the hell?" Melvin mumbled to himself.

Dave reached for the light switch and switched it to the "on" position, but nothing happened.

Dave looked at Melvin and whispered, "I guess this is going to be your room. At least you won't have to paint."

Both men stepped out of the room giggling.

"Who in the hell paints a room bright pink like that?" Melvin grunted.

"Maybe that's just one more side of ole' Uncle Cleve that you didn't know about, and what's up with all that old stuff in there? It was like George Washington himself has been sleepin' in there."

"Hell, he slept everywhere else didn't he? Talk 'bout a freak! Every time you pass an old ass hotel or inn you see 'George Washington slept here' and you know a guy that walked around in a wig all day definitely did a whole lot of fuckin' all night! Had to re-establish his manhood, you know? Boy, I bet that there are more stains from old George's nut sack on more bed sheets than you could shake a stick at, the nasty presidential bastard! You know, if I close my eyes half shut and stare at you, you look like you could be related to old George. You could be his long lost great, great, great grandson's cousin's, sister's, nephew's brother-in-law's, uncle's, left God-son's wench's son."

"Yeah, and you look like you were conceived through masturbation! I can still see welt marks on your forehead! But what has that got to do with this room bein' pink? Maybe Uncle Cleve had a woman livin' here or somethin' 'cause you know he was an old freak, too!"

Dave shrugged his shoulders and continued laughing.

"Maybe it was Uncle Cleve's and the crazy stank ho from next door's freak room!"

Looking as grossed out as he possibly could, Melvin turned and pointed at Dave. "WHATEVA!"

They continued checking out the rest of the house and then headed for the car. Before getting in, both men glanced over at the fence. With Marie nowhere in sight, the men climbed into the car.

Heading down the driveway, their exit was quickly blocked by metal, rubber, and smoke. Melvin stopped the vehicle and stepped out. Dave remained inside, listening to the radio and tapping on the dashboard. It was an old pickup truck reminiscent of *Sanford and Son.*

"Excuse me!"

"Yo man, excuse us, we're tryin' to get by and you're blockin' the way!"

Seconds later, the door opened. A small Latino man stepped down from the truck's opening onto the ground.

"Buenos Dias."

"Yeah, buwavo deego to you too, uh can I help you?"

"I am Mr. Carlos. Carlos Lopez. I am, how you say, de handymon. Choo live here now?"

Melvin glanced over at the truck. He could see rakes, and lawn mowers and other tools in the back of the truck bed.

"Uh yeah, this is me. If you're lookin' to get paid for cuttin' the grass or somethin', that aint got nothin' to do with me. You have to take that up with Mr. Salter."

Mr. Carlos leaned back and put up both his hands.

"No, no. I see the car so I come in. I was thinking if you need handymon. I can do for choo. I can cut grass, paint, fix things, choo know? What ever choo need."

Melvin stood there listening to the little man go on about all of his skills and abilities. He was like a one-man neighborhood maintenance crew. After he was done, Melvin started back towards the car.

"Come see me tomorrow and we'll talk about some things that need doing. Oh yeah, my name is Melvin. I gotta go right now, but we'll talk tomorrow. Alright?"

Mr. Carlos opened the door to the truck and yelled back, "Sure thing Señor Malveen, sure thing. I come back manana-tomorrow."

He drove the smoking contraption over towards the fence and Melvin sped by. After reaching the road, Melvin looked over at Dave.

"Some handyman, if he was any kind of handyman, he'd fix that raggedy ass truck of his."

"Man you know that there is no such thing. A handyman with a nice truck, that's like being a professional hockey player and having all your teeth."

"Yeah, I guess you're right. It's like making a good steak and cheese sub in a nice, clean fancy restaurant."

"Food, it's always food with you."

Melvin shrugged his shoulders, waited for the traffic to clear then pulled off.

CHAPTER 9   THE MOVE

The next morning, Melvin made the necessary calls to the water, electric, and gas-companies and changed his address at the post office. He had called his old friend Cedric who worked at "Freeland's Florist" after he had gotten home the night before. Cedric had agreed to use the company's van to move Melvin's things. Melvin had also gotten some of the teenage boys from the neighborhood to help with the move and of course, supervisor Dave would be there.

While in the process of packing up his kitchen utensils, he heard a knock at the door. "Must be the Cedric," he thought to himself. Melvin slid the box marked "Kitchen" to the other side of the counter on which it laid. He opened up the door.

"Man you're early."

Melvin's facial expression changed after he realized that it wasn't Cedric at the door. To his surprise, there she stood, all five feet, ten inches of her. It was Wendy.

"Uh, wasup lady? What are you doin' here, and how did you know where I live?"

Wendy stood there with her hands stuffed down in her tan trench coat pockets.

"Are you gonna make me stand out in the hall all day?"

"My bad Baby, yeah – come on in!"

Melvin opened the door wider then stepped out of the entranceway. Wendy stepped into the apartment giving the place the once over.

"Nice place Mel, moving?"

Melvin walked over and sat on one of the bar stools in front of the breakfast nook. Wendy sat on the couch and crossed her legs showing a hint of her thigh.

"Yeah, I'm movin', but never mind that, what brings you on my side of town?"

Wendy pushed herself further back on the couch and folded her hands in her lap. "Well Mel, I heard that you quit your job the other day. I also heard that security officers escorted you out because you attacked Mr. Carr. All this happened right after you left my office. I don't know if I had upset you to the point that you took your frustration out on someone else. I hope I wasn't the cause, but just in case I was, I came to apologize, and offer to make it up to you somehow."

Melvin stood up and walked over to the couch. He looked down at Wendy smiling and brushing the dust from his pant leg. He thought about her being there and the reason she stated. He knew that she had other motives for coming down to his cracker box rat hole and being so nice. He thought, "This gold diggin' wench must think I just fell off the stupid wagon. Yeah right, apologize my ass, but bein' the common dog that I am, let's see how far she'll go with this."

Melvin sat next to the woman and placed his left arm behind her shoulders resting it on the back of the couch. "You're right. I just couldn't take the rejection that day. I just snapped. After I left you, I was so angry. I was angry at you, angry at me, I was angry at the world. I felt rejected and disappointed. You made me feel so low. Like, I wasn't good enough for you or anybody else. I just wanted to love you girl, that's all. I guess I lost it after you made it so clear that it was never gonna happen."

Melvin paused for a second then leaned over and whispered in her ear, "But, I can think of a million ways for you to make it up to me. You know you're all I ever think about. How about you and me right now, stretched out on this couch, sweatin' and smilin'? You can save me from myself, from therapy even."

Now Melvin had taken his right hand and placed it on her thigh. He moved his hand up higher very slowly. Wendy reached down and placed her hand on top of his to slyly prevent him from reaching his always forbidden zone. Melvin then quickly skimmed through the "playas manual" that he kept stored in his half empty mind. He stopped on quick reference page 56. With his left hand already behind her, he placed his hand on the left side of Wendy's face and pushed it towards him. As their eyes met, Melvin quickly pressed his lips against hers and jammed his tongue in her mouth. He knew it was an old 1976 move, but what the hell, this might have been his only chance. Wendy's hands sunk into the soft flesh that gathered around Melvin's shoulders in an attempt to push him off of her. As soon as she touched his shoulders, he pushed his hand deep into her crotch and started wiggling his middle finger searching for an opening.

"Damn, Melvin, hold it!"

Melvin ignored her and continued his pawing.

"Calm down. C'mon now baby, there will be plenty of time for that. If you've been waiting this long, waiting just a little while longer won't matter. Don't you want it to be right? I don't want to be laid down over a bunch of boxes. I want you too, Baby, just not like this."

Wendy's act was so unconvincing, but still, Melvin did not care. He was going to keep the pressure on. He leaned back on the couch with his legs wide open. Wendy had noticed the little teepee that had erected itself during his attempted conquest. Melvin looked down at the pulled pointed fabric of his dusty sweatpants.

"You see what you've done to me woman? Why you stop? Couldn't you feel the chemistry? C'mon girl, save me. Please save me!"

Wendy stood up and started adjusting her clothes. I guess her greed had its boundaries. She was willing to do whatever she needed, but on her terms.

"Melvin, there's a time and a place for everything. I don't have enough time right now, Baby. Don't you want it to be right? We can get together after you're all settled in at your new place. I know you want it to be right, too."

Melvin rolled over on his side and began tugging on his erection.

"Sheeeeeit girl, right now couldn't be any righter! You feelin' me, right? I'm feelin' you. What's up? You can give me a sample right now and put in some real work after I'm moved in. You know, do the movie and dinner thing and follow up with an all nighter. So how 'bout a quickie?"

Wendy said nothing. She gathered herself and started for the door. She turned back and blew Melvin a kiss.

"Yeah, I'm feeling you honey, but later. I'm not into quickies. I'm a passionate woman who's into passionate love making. I want us to be able to take our time. I need foreplay, Baby. You can't just jump on me like a rabbit and pump me like I'm some kind of inflatable doll. Call me after you've moved and have gotten all settled in. Then we'll continue this conversation. I do want to make things up to you, really." She turned and headed for the door.

As she approached the door, two loud knocks rang out. "KNOCK! KNOCK!" Melvin lifted himself off the couch and tried adjusting the all too obvious bulge that didn't seem to want to deflate.

"You want me to get that?" Wendy asked.

"Hold up! Give me a sec. It's probably the movers."

Melvin reached over and picked up the empty box off of the counter and positioned it in front of his crotch to hide his embarrassment. The empty box tilted up at a funny angle as it was resting on top of an unusually unlevel surface.

"Okay, you can open it. It's the movers and they're here for this box."

Wendy, giggling, opened the door and walked right past Dave without saying a word.

"Well good morning to you, too Baby, damn! Wit your fine ass! I'm buyin' whatever you're sellin'."

Dave stepped through the door.

"Damn man, who's that?"

Dave had never met Wendy, but had heard a million stories about her from Melvin who was now motioning for him to quickly close the door. He walked over and flopped down on the couch but kept the box securely on his lap. It still had a slight incline.

"That's her man, that's Wendy, my lady and ... I was just about to tax that ass, until you came bangin' on the door like the damn police."

"Yeah right. If that's your lady, how come I never met her? I mean, I've never met your other lady either, but that's because you keep her hidden in her box. You say you were gettin' ready to hit that huh? Yeah right! Oh you mean, as in gettin' ready to hit her over the head and knock her into unconsciousness, tap that ass and then leave the country. Bein' your boy and all, and as phat as she was ... I could be an accomplice. Hell, I hear Mexico's nice this time of year."

Melvin walked over to Dave and stuck his middle finger in front of his face.

"You don't believe me? Then smell my finger."

Dave revved back and produced an ugly frown on his face. He placed his index finger under his nose, and tried to speak while coughing.

"No thanks, I'm tryin' to quit. I'm sure it smells great though. Hey, you been fryin' fish or boilin' sewer water?"

"Very funny. Not my lady though. She douches that ass twice a day. She keeps it fresh for me. You know why? Huh? Do you know why my brotha?"

Melvin paused for several seconds then sniffed his middle finger once more. He then looked back at Dave and started to speak, but was cut off by Dave yelling, "Because a ho never knows!"

Dave looked around the room. He noticed nothing had been moved and there was a lot of packing left to do.

"So what you gone do, burn all of this worthless shit?"

Melvin lifted the box and placed it back on the counter.

"Nah, Cedric's on his way with the van. We're gone hopefully move everything in one haul. I've got some young backs comin', too."

Dave walked over and rummaged through the box.

"Whatcha takin' all this old stuff for? Why you takin' this old junk to your new house? Melvin, you've got the money, start fresh man! All you're gone do is haul all this crap over there just to throw it out lata. Why don't you save yourself some time? Throw this crap out now! It's bad enough you've got all that Civil War junk to get rid of as it is. Let me see here … Yep, as I look around, all I see is crap. Crap! Crap! And even more crap!"

Melvin looked at Dave for a second and then around the room.

"Damn, you're right man. I guess I could buy some new things. Well it would be hard to find another piece of shit toaster, where only one side works, but I gotta keep my Bruce Lee on velvet, and my TV with the coat hanger and automatic pliers channel changer! Ok, you're right; I can replace all of this crap!"

Dave picked up the phone and handed it to Melvin.

"Don't you want to call the Salvation Army first?"

"Nah, I'll just get Cedric to run it all over there. Where in the hell is he anyway? Hold on a sec. Let me see if he's out front."

Melvin grabbed his jacket and keys and then headed out the door. He stepped out on the landing of the entrance and looked up and down the street.

"I saw that lady going up. She's was real fine lookin', too."

It was Mr. Belger, or better known as "Walt", the maintenance man. He was a nice guy, but extremely nosey. He would sit in his ground floor apartment and watch everybody who came in and out of the building. Then he would go to the peep hole of his front door to see what apartment they were going to. He would even open his front door to watch them as they went up to the upstairs apartments. He was a southern man from Salisbury, North Carolina. He always used that deep southern slang that made Melvin laugh.

Oddly, Walt had this uncanny gift. He could somehow always remember past incidents, and could describe what each individual's fashion statement was on that particular day. That's right; he could remember what each person was wearing on the day the incident took place. Well, that's what he led us all to believe anyway. No one could dispute his descriptions because no one else could remember.

Walt never liked Dave though. He always said that Dave would one day get Melvin into trouble. He knew that Dave could be mean as a snake!

"Hey Walt. How you doin' this mornin'? Sure is a nice day aint it?"

"Well Mel, I'm fair ta middlin' and yep, this day is shapin' up real fine. So who is she?"

"Oh her, that's just my new lady."

"Well I'll be dipt in butta milk! Wow Mel, how'd you snag a gul likat? I mean, she had some gams on her, too! She wuz showin' off dem fat legs wit dat toit short skoirt. That toit shoirt looked real good round her, too. Have ya drank her baf wotta yet?"

"What in the hell does that mean, Walt?"

"You tasted that honey yet, you know?"

"Oh you mean have I licked that thing yet? Nah man, eatin' that thing gives me gas! And that's kinda embarrassin' when you're down there between a woman's legs and you blow one. Kinda knocks the mood if you know what I mean."

"Damn boy, you aint supposed to eat 'til ya full. That's the first time I've ever heard of anythang such. Well I saw somethin' on the television yesday dat might help ya. What's dat thang called? Oh yeah, dat's it, BENO! Like they say, take BENO for ya eat, and dere won't BE-NO gas lata!

I memba a friend da mine back in da day, his name wuz Joe. We wuz down at dis ole juke joint and he met dis big old Chinee gul. She had some fat long legs and hair down to hu sit down. She wasn't like most dem. She was a biggen'. She was tall and thick, you know big boned and fat tattys, too. Her daddy owned da only Chinee restrant in Salisbury. So ta git at hu was all he wanted. It was like dat tabu kinda thang. He was wearing his favit green slakes, some of dose cool gray silk socks and his new wing tipped toed shoes wit a black shoirt. You know the kind wit dem long collas? Oh he was struttin' it alright.

She had on a short skoirt, if memry serves me right, it was blue. She had on a white blouse wit ruffles on front too, showin' dem two biggens. Ole Joe did everythang he could ta git atta. He musta courted dat gul for months for she give in. Finely, dat boy Joe wuz fiddin' ta lay down wit dat ole Chinee gul dat he'd bin wontin' for a long while. He finally got his chance. Just win he wuz bout ta sticka wit da ole hot beef injection, he farted. I mean dat boy tode me dat it sounded like one of dem sonic booms but only wet. Yeah, dat fixed his li'l red wagon. He say dat ole gul jumped up and lef smoke. She must bin one of dem ninjas, cuz she disappeared. He neva did git his chance wit hu agin! So I say dat ta say dis… you gotta watch ya farts Melvin."

Melvin laughed at Walt's suggestion, but Walt was as serious as ever.

"That's funny Walt, real funny, but I don't think that BENO will work for that."

"Well ok, but it's work a try. Hey, I also seen dat fella, you know, dat friend of yorn. What he do, run yo lady friend off? I still say dat boy is crooked as a dog's hind leg and mean, too. Told me if I kept bein' so nosey, he was gonna rip out my eyes and he wont joshin', either."

"Nah, he was just messin' with you Walt."

Melvin could hear the car doors slam and the squeaky voice yelling.

"There he is, that's the motha fucka right there!"

Walt closed his window and drew his curtains shut. He was nosey, but in no need of trouble.

Advancing toward Melvin was two big angry looking men trailed by a small petite woman. It was the librarian, Cheryl from the other night. She was walking behind the two large men yelling at the top of her lungs.

"Yeah, that's his ass. Him and his buddy threw me out of the car and left me after trying to rape me! Kick his ass!"

"Hey hold on now, it wasn't me. You must have me mixed up with my twin brother. He's the one who likes to hang out at night. Did you meet him at The Sapphi…"

The men snatched Melvin from the steps and threw him onto the sidewalk. Melvin continued trying to convince them that this was a case of mistaken identity. They weren't buying his lie. One of the men stood over him and was getting ready to stomp his head when a voice spoke calmly.

"Is there a problem here?"

It was Dave. He was standing in the doorway with both of his hands stuffed in the pockets of his jeans with his shirt wide open displaying his white tank top tee shirt and his nine millimeter hand gun neatly tucked into his pants. The men turned and slowly backed up with their hands raised.

"If the man said it wasn't him, then it wasn't him," continued Dave.

"It was him, it was both of you!" The woman shouted.

"Bitch I got a twin, too, must have been both of our twins. They're both assholes."

Cheryl seemed to be the only one not afraid of Dave's gun. She continued to yell as they eased back to their car.

"You gone pay for what you did. I'm gone get both of you… and your damn twins if that be the case. You gone pay!"

Cheryl and the two huge men piled back into the car and sped off. Melvin slowly picked himself up off the hard pavement and began brushing himself off. Dave smiled then turned and walked back upstairs. Melvin started back up the steps to his apartment building. He heard Walt's window open slowly. With his curtains still drawn, Melvin could hear his voice whisper.

"Mean as a snake dat boy is."

Before Melvin could enter the building, a white van pulled up to the curb. The tall lean figure jumped out and waved over to Mel.

"Sorry I'm late man, the boss…" Melvin cut Cedric's excuse short.

"Look here man, you bein' late almost got my ass killed, so let's roll. I've got some of the young boys comin'. Here's the key to the front door. Red Mike, Mark, and Lil Griss should be here any minute. Tell them to load everything up, and help you deliver it to the 'Goodwill' or the 'Salvation Army', whichever is closest. Here's five bills. Give them a hundred a piece and you keep the rest."

Cedric nodded his head in agreement and headed toward the front steps to the building.

Melvin called up to Dave, "Dave, let's go man!"

The curtains were opened again and once again Walt's face appeared.

"Melvin, what's up, you fiddin ta move'?"

"Yeah, I'm getting' away from this dump man. You see how crazy folks are around here, so much violence man, just too much violence. I'm just too tender for this shit."

"Well maybe you shouldn't have lef dat young lady out dere by huself da ova evenin'. What if somefin' had happened to hu Mel? You wouldn't have been able to live wit dat."

Melvin stood there thinking. He didn't even think about her safety that night. He felt bad. Realizing that Walt had made a valid point he acknowledged him.

"Shut the hell up Walt, I said it wasn't me! Dave, come on man!"

Dave came walking down the steps with a big box. Melvin held the door for him as he came out. Walt's curtains were again closed.

"Man, I thought you said that I shouldn't take any of my junk to the new place?"

"Yeah, I know, which means that you won't be needin' this 'George Foreman' grill or your juicer and I found a few other things that I could use, too."

"What kind of bullshit is that?"

"You won't need it. Cedric's up there now goin' through the rest. Do you actually think that half of your shit is gone make it to the Salvation Army? Not! You know he's gone sell all your shit and whatever he can't sell will be thrown in the nearest dumpster."

Melvin started back towards the door, but Dave stepped over and blocked the entrance.

"Let the man make a few dollars, after all, he did sneak the van from his job to help your ass out. Let it go man. Everybody's got to hustle."

Melvin stopped and looked at Dave. He looked up the stairs and then turned.

"Let's go man."

Melvin and Dave walked to the car. Melvin popped the trunk to the Escort and Dave placed the box inside. They climbed in the car and headed to the furniture store.

After four hours of shopping, Melvin decided that it was time to replace the Escort. They headed to the car dealership where he purchased a new BMW 745. He offered to buy Dave a new ride as well, but Dave declined his offer.

Before heading out to Mount Vernon, Melvin decided to ride through the neighborhood to show off his new ride. While driving, they saw the florist van parked on Benning Road and Cedric standing at the back of the van, selling merchandise from the Melvin Dossier Collection.

Dave laughed.

"Hey man, pull over. I see a nice one sided toaster. I wonder how much he's selling that for."

Melvin didn't respond. He cut his neighborhood cruise short and headed for Virginia.

CHAPTER 10   THE ROOM

Melvin sat quietly in the kitchen at the small table near the window, enjoying a hot cup of coffee and the view outside. He looked around the house and smiled to himself.

"I can't believe it's been a month already."

He was truly satisfied with himself and his new life. This feeling, he had never felt before. Everything was just about done. He had purchased his furniture, had the entire lower level painted and Mr. Carlos was now upstairs finishing up the upper level. He had all of that disgusting old antique furniture removed, and auctioned off. He actually made a sizable profit from it. As he sipped from his mug, he could hear Mr. Carlos walk down the steps, through the front of the house and into the kitchen.

"Señor Malveen, I have put three coats of paint on the walls of the back bedroom, but the original pink, it come back. Choo come see, Señor Malveen. Choo come see."

Melvin placed his mug on the table and followed Mr. Carlos upstairs. Melvin stood with his hands on his hips and his mouth wide open.

"What the...? Are you sure you painted this room?"

Melvin looked around and saw the paint brushes and rollers covered with the new colored paint. He saw the opened paint cans and drippings of the same color on the drop cloths.

"Si, I paint."

"Well what happened? What else can we do?"

Mr. Carlos stepped inside the room placing his hand on the wall and rubbing it.

"What to do? I can try more primer, but I already use two can of that. This is the first time that I ever see anyting like thees.

I no sure of what kind of paint they use, but the primer just won't go on. What about some wallpaper?"

Mr. Carlos bent down to straighten up the drop cloths that he had spread all over the floor. Melvin continued looking around the room in amazement.

"I guess anything beats this crap. Let's take a quick ride over to the 'Sherwood Willis' store and see what they have."

After realizing he meant "Sherwin-Williams," Mr. Carlos nodded in agreement. He remained quiet and decided that it wasn't worth correcting. He started placing the lids onto the opened paint cans. Pulling out the rag that was hanging from the back pocket of his overalls, he leaned over and picked up one of the paintbrushes lying on top of one of the empty cans.

"Give me one minute Señor Malveen, I be right there."

Mr. Carlos collected all of his paintbrushes, and rollers. He followed Melvin back downstairs and proceeded to the basement. He began cleaning his brushes in the wash sink. As he washed the pink paint from his brush, he noticed that the paint running into the drain was not pink. It wasn't pink, or the gray color of the primer that he had used earlier. It was black. It was the deepest, darkest black that he had ever seen.

"Señor Malveen! Señor Malveen!" Mr. Carlos screamed out.

Melvin walked over to the top of the stairs leading to the basement.

"Yeah, what is it now?"

He looked down into the dim light, and saw Mr. Carlos waving him down.

"You must see," he whispered.

Melvin made his way down the basement steps and followed Mr. Carlos to the washtub where he still had the water running.

"What's up? Don't tell me the paint has messed up your brushes too."

Melvin looked into the tub. Mr. Carlos pointed to the blackness slithering its way down the wash drain.

"You called me to come watch you clean your brushes? Man, I don't have time for this."

Mr. Carlos pointed to the pink paint on top of the brush and then over to the black liquid. "It starts out pink then it turns black."

"Man, you gotta stop using those cheap ass brushes. How you gonna give quality work using shit like that. Come on, I'll pick you up some new ones while we're out."

"But Señor Malveen, you don't understand, they are good brushes, new ones too!"

Melvin looked down at the black substance once more and turned to walk away.

"Cheap ass paint then. Let's roll!"

Mr. Carlos placed the remaining brushes in the small bucket that he used to store them. He made his way back upstairs and out the door where he found Melvin waiting. They climbed into Melvin's brand new BMW and headed off to the paint store.

He was leaning in front of a large bright yellow counter displaying his large name tag pinned to his short white smock. His thin black framed glasses sat comfortably on the edge of his nose. His long thick bushy hair was filled with grey and pushed back displaying his pushed out forehead. Wrinkles covered the lower section of his face and the top of his forehead as well. His grey slacks were snug fitting and hung just above the neatly tied strings of his Hush Puppies.

"Good afternoon gents, and what can I help you with today?" He asked smiling cheerfully.

Melvin looked over at Mr. Carlos who immediately spoke up.

"Some paint. We need some paint for inside."

"And none of that cheap stuff either. We need some heavy-duty stuff. You carry that?" Melvin interjected.

The store clerk reached up and slid his glasses off of his nose. He nodded and extended his hand toward the back of the store. "Heavy duty, well you've come to the right place. Follow me gents."

He led them over to a big wooden counter that was positioned in front of the large storefront window. On the counter lay huge books filled with wallpaper and border samples. Six tall barstools were scattered along the front of the counter with cushioned round pads covered in plaid burlap material.

"Have a seat over here gentleman. Do we know what the color scheme is or would you like to just look through some swatches?'

"Swatches?" Melvin asked. "Man, I didn't come in here to look at no damn Swatches! Look, you gone have to get your little hustle on at another time. We need paint! And besides, I don't wear no damn Swatch. Look at this here Cuz. This here is a Rolex. So why would I want to buy a cheap ass Swatch, huh?"

"No, no sir. I mean some of our fabric and paint color samples! We call them swatches."

Melvin slid his sleeve over his shiny gaudy watch and opened one of the large books in front of him trying to hide his embarrassment. The man only smiled and Mr. Carlos had no idea what was going on. He was amazed at all the different textures and colors that were displayed in the large books.

"Uh yeah, that'll be good. Yeah, let's have a look at those swatches."

The clerk disappeared then quickly returned with another book and several boards with little plastic strips of all different colors on them.

"This is just a few samples of our highest quality paints, but there are other brands and assorted colors over there on the wall."

He directed the men's attention to another wall on the other side of the store, but neither man rose from his seat. Melvin opened the book and Mr. Carlos leaned in to get a closer look.

"This is your best, or as you said, your highest quality stuff, huh?"

"Yes sir, guaranteed not to fade or peel for ten years!" The clerk boasted.

Melvin turned a few pages and then stopped about a third of the way through the book. He paused for a second then squinted his eyes toward the color chart on the other side of the room. Too lazy to get up, Melvin turned the book so that the clerk could view his color selection.

"Give me this color right here. How many coats will we need to cover over a pink wall?"

"Is the wall primed?"

"Oh yeah, my man here has been primin' the hell out of it, but it still won't hold that pink back."

"Well sir, with a good primer, this paint here will only require one coat. Without a primer though, I'd say two and maybe a light third if you have any bleeding areas at all."

Melvin stood up and handed the book back to the clerk. He placed his hand on Mr. Carlos' shoulder and stuck two fingers out in front of him signifying two cans. Mr. Carlos nodded in agreement.

"We'll take two gallons of the Solomon Beige and give us a couple of gallons of that good primer too. As a matter of fact, I like this wallpaper here. Give me enough rolls to cover an 11x15 room. I'll get the paint as backup."

"Yes sir." The clerk acknowledged, and off he went.

After returning from the closed door that read "Employees Only", the clerk carried two gallon cans labeled "White Base" to the big machine located in the back of the store. He pried the lid off of one and placed it underneath the nozzle that hung from the top of the machine. He pressed several buttons and pulled the side lever down which caused the machine to dispense a small amount of color from the nozzle.

After replacing the lid, the clerk put the can in a metal drum that also had a few buttons and a switch located on top. He shut the metal door, pressed one of the buttons and pushed the switch to the "on" position. The metal drum made a loud banging noise as it shook the paint container then began to hum quietly.

Once the metal drum came to a stop and began beeping, the clerk repeated this same process for the other can of paint. He proceeded to the front counter carrying two cans in each hand where he placed them in front of the cash register. He left the men at the register for a few minutes more only to return from the stock room with several rolls of the wallpaper Melvin had selected.

"Will that be all for you today gents?"

Melvin reached into the back pocket of his trousers and retrieved his wallet.

"You need anything else Carlos? Glue, brushes?"

He started pulling out some of the bills from one of the compartments of his wallet.

"No, that should do it. Are choo sure choo want wallpaper first?"

"Yeah, this should cover the wall pretty good. We should have thought of this first. If it works alright, I'll just bring the paint back. I can return this if I don't need it, right?"

The clerk picked up the contraption that lay next to the register. It was one of those gray scanners with the black plate in front that resembled an electric shaver. He ran the scanner over the bar codes of each item and hit the "total" button.

"Of course, just bring it back with your receipt and we'll take care of it. Ok, that'll be $407.43"

"407? Damn, does it come with a rebate too?"

The clerk smile and push up his glasses, "You said you wanted the best. This is the best!"

Melvin passed the clerk four crisp one hundred dollar bills and a twenty. After placing it in the drawer, the clerk passed him back his change and a receipt. He reached into the container sitting on the counter and retrieved a small pamphlet and some wooden sticks to stir the paint.

"This'll tell you all about the paint and how to apply it and things of that nature."

"Oh nah man, we won't be needin' that. My man here is a professional."

Melvin picked up the shopping bag filled with the wallpaper and the sticks. Mr. Carlos grabbed two of the cans and nodded, then headed for the door. The clerk rushed from behind the counter and opened the door for both men. He followed them to the car carrying the two cans of primer still reassuring them on how fine the products were they had just purchased. Once at the car, the clerk leaned over to whisper to Melvin.

"My man, you like DVDs? I got it all. Anything you need, and they're clear, too. Got CDs, too."

Melvin looked over to Mr. Carlos and then back at the clerk.

"Slim, look here," Melvin whispered. "Didn't I tell you that you were gonna have to get your hustle on at another time?"

"This is another time! I'm just trying to do you a solid, man. C'mon brotha, just tell me what you need."

Melvin pushed a button on his remote to unlock the car and pop the trunk. Mr. Carlos placed the cans of paint, primer and paper inside the trunk. Both men started for the doors as the clerk followed Melvin.

"I've got those XXX joints, the new Denzel, I even got the new R. Kelly jam. That hasn't even been released yet. You know that cut 'The Younga the Betta'. Got it! What you need?"

Melvin stopped at the car, and turned to face the clerk. He pushed his hands deep into his pockets and let out a deep sigh.

"What do I need? Let's see, what do I need? I think I'll start with you gettin' your Hush Puppy, pin stripe silk sock, bowlin' slacked, too small barber shop smock, thick soda bottle bifocal, Linc from Mod Squad half bush, half 'Ready for the World' jheri curl wearin', over fifty too damn old to be doin' this kind of shit DVD peddlin' ass out of my face. Now that's what I need! So if you don't mind?"

The clerk stood there as if he were waiting for Melvin to break out into laughter. After a few seconds, he mumbled, "Damn, that's cold bro."

He slowly turned and headed for the store. After reaching the curb, he turned and looked back towards the car. At this time, Melvin was just beginning to roll down the dark tinted window of his BMW just enough to stick out his middle finger. The men pulled off.

Upon their return, Mr. Carlos went right to work. He covered each wall of the room with the wallpaper that Melvin had purchased from the paint store. That would be the "Sherwin-Williams", of course.

Hours later, after he was done, Mr. Carlos called Melvin upstairs to inspect the work. Melvin walked upstairs and down the hall to the room. He was holding a large glass filled with a beverage and cramming a sandwich into his mouth. He could hear Mr. Carlos gathering all of his supplies, as he got closer to the room. Melvin stepped into the room and started smiling and pointing his sandwich at Mr. Carlos.

"Now that's what in the hell I'm talkin' 'bout!"

The room no longer had the bright, but dreary looking pink colored paint glowing throughout. It no longer had the antique furniture or the dark window shutters shielding the sunlight. It was now warm and cozy looking. The wallpaper was tan with thin navy blue stripes, and what appeared to be anchors, randomly placed throughout.

Melvin took a sip from his drink then wiped his mouth on his shirt.

"When can you do the floors?"

Mr. Carlos continued to pull up the drop cloth up from the floor.

"Tomorrow, if choo wish."

Melvin took another bite from his huge sandwich, and looked around the room again. He was very impressed and already visualizing how he was going to turn it into his game room.

"Cool, tomorrow will be real cool. I'll order the curtains and furniture tomorrow, too."

As Mr. Carlos walked by him holding the crumpled up drop cloth under his arm, Melvin looked around once more then placed his hand on Mr. Carlos's shoulder.

"You da man!"

Mr. Carlos smiled and headed for his old Ford pickup truck that was sitting out front of the house. After packing up his equipment and tools, Mr. Carlos climbed into his truck, waved to Melvin, who was now standing on the porch eating a chunk of cake. Melvin watched Mr. Carlos pull off and exit through the gate.

"Hey Baby! Yoo-hoooooo, Melvin!"

Melvin looked around, but could see no one in sight. It was just starting to get dark outside, but was light enough to see a person standing in speaking range.

"Hey handsome!"

Melvin then recognized the voice. It was Marie from next door, but her voice wasn't coming from the fence this time. Over the past month, she would occasionally stand by the fence at all times of day or night and yell obscenities at him.

"Where is she?"

Melvin looked up and down the wrought iron fence that separated their yards, and then the voice became louder and closer.

"How about a little suckie fuckie, huh neighbor?"

Melvin stepped down onto the top step of the porch. He saw the thin shadow making its way up the driveway, his driveway.

"Take your nasty ass home Marie. You're trespassin' or should I say ho-passin'."

"I was just trying to catch Carlos before he left. I saw him leaving out and thought I'd meet him by the gate. He slowed down, but as I got closer he sped off. That fool almost ran me over. I didn't even know that old clunker of his could move that fast. He probably didn't know that it was me waving him down, because he would have stopped for me. I find Latin men just as sexy as you African American studs!"

Melvin inched his way towards the front door. He continued to yell to Marie as she made her way towards the front porch. "He probably wanted to run your nasty ass over! What do you want anyway?"

Marie's silhouette drew nearer. Melvin could see her frail body making its way up the driveway. Walking at a snail's pace, she continued yelling. "I'm here to borrow a few things neighbor. I've run out next door and haven't had a chance to run out and pick any up. I was going out the get some yesterday, but that old buzzard in there was acting up. I tried to catch Carlos to get it from him, but he seemed to be in quite a hurry."

"Well hurry up, I've got things to do woman. What do you need? A cup a sugar?"

Marie slowly advanced up the steps. She grabbed on to the wooden plank railing to assist her climb. As the porch light slightly shined against her pale face, she looked up at Melvin and spoke calmly. She pulled up the sleeve of her thick blue knitted sweater just above her wrist and held out her hand. Melvin could barely hear her crackly voice say, "Some stiff hot meat!"

Melvin stepped back into the house whispering, "Nasty bitch!" and slammed his door.

The next morning, there was a knock at the door. Melvin rolled over and looked at the clock that was sitting on his new cherry wood nightstand. 9:18 displayed on its face.

"Must be Mr. Carlos."

Melvin sat up on the side of the bed, picked up his pants off the floor and slipped them on. He walked down to the door and opened it.

"Rise and shine, Cinderella."

Dave stood there with a big grin on his face. He looked Melvin up and down with a look of disgust. Melvin stood there with his eyes half opened.

"Move man, let me in."

Dave grunted while pushing Melvin out of his way and stepping inside. "Damn, I didn't even hear the cab pull up."

Just as Melvin was about to shut the door, he could hear Mr. Carlos's pickup truck racing up the driveway. It was clicking and back firing as usual. His loud Latin music blared up the driveway and then shut off as he came to a halt.

"Damn, y'all some early birds."

Mr. Carlos jumped out, walked around the back of the truck and immediately started pulling his tools out from the truck bed. Melvin pushed the door open and Dave stepped aside. Mr. Carlos bounced through the door.

"Buenos dias!" he shouted in his usual cheery voice.

"Yeah, uh, deez nuts to you too, amigo!" mumbled Dave.

Melvin stepped up and pushed the door closed after Mr. Carlos completed dragging in all of his equipment. He turned and looked at Mr. Carlos, smiling. "Man, you almost did your civil and just duty yesterday amigo."

"Huh? What do choo mean?" Mr. Carlos asked with a puzzled look.

"You damn near killed the bitch! That's what you did, would've done the world a favor, too. Man we need to work on your drivin' skills though. You can't miss somebody that close. Next time focus more!"

The men began to laugh. Dave looking confused couldn't help to ask, "Run over? Run over, who?"

Melvin shook his thumb towards the direction of Marie's house. Dave began to laugh.

"Not that crazy scab infested thing from next door?"

They all began to laugh even harder with that. Mr. Carlos continued laughing as well. He twisted his painter's cap towards the back as he began to speak loudly.

"Si, Si, Señor Melveene! She got the scabs, and the crabs too! Ella puede aspirar un pene también"

Melvin and Dave looked at each other, but continued to laugh.

Dave finally asked, "What in the hell does that mean man?"

Mr. Carlos bending over his tools looked up at the guys and smiled.

"How do choo say? The lady, yeah, the lady, she's good with dee mouth, too!"

Mr. Carlos picked up his tools, turned and then carried them upstairs to the back room to begin working on the floors.

Both men stopped laughing as they looked at each other. Dave produced his deadliest frown. It was as if he had just bitten into the world's sourest lemon.

"Oh, no he didn't! Tell me that man did not just say that he let the next doe stank ho slob his rod. Say it isn't so, and he's still alive. His ass probably itches a lot I bet. Maybe he was workin' on a green card. Nah, my ass would just have to stay in Cuba or Mexico or wherever the hell he's from."

"You want some coffee man?"

Melvin pointed to the kitchen. Dave turned and headed in that direction. Melvin followed.

"I can't eat or drink after hearin' that shit. Damn, that little nasty motha fucka! Yuk!"

Melvin chuckled as he entered the kitchen. The sound of the tools hitting the hardwood floors rang out like a small explosion.

"Santa Maria!" Mr. Carlos shouted.

"He must have just had a flash back!" Dave yelled out. "He must have just realized that he actually slept with that hag."

Both men rushed upstairs to see what had happened. Mr. Carlos was standing there with both of his hands on his face as he started backing out of the room. Melvin was marching toward the room.

"What? What happened?"

Mr. Carlos tried to speak, but couldn't. He backed out of the room, turned, looked at Melvin and could only point to the inside of the room. Melvin stepped into the room, followed by Dave. Melvin placed his hand over his mouth and shook his head in disbelief. It was as if nothing had been done to the room at all. All of the wallpaper was gone. It was as if it had never been hung. The glue was even wiped clean. The pink paint was even more vivid than before and the ceiling that was the only thing that held the white paint, had reverted back to its original dull faded off-white color.

Dave walked into the room. He looked at Melvin standing there with his still shocked look on his face.

"Why you trippin'? I told you that this was an ugly ass color!" and walked back out.

Melvin slowly backed out of the room and rushed down the stairs followed by Mr. Carlos. Dave, unaware of the bewilderment of both men, slowly made his way back downstairs.

Out on the front porch, Mr. Carlos paced back and forth along the plank floor, with his hands on his hips. Still looking on in disbelief, he turned to Melvin.

"Señor Malveen, I no understand. This no right."

Melvin leaned back through the doorway and looked back up the stairs. He walked over to Mr. Carlos and placed his hands on the railing beside him.

"Maybe the paint had some bad chemicals in it, or maybe the wallpaper was old or somethin'."

"No, Señor Malveen, it is the same paint that I always use. Se frecuenta este lugar, se frecuenta este lugar!"

He rushed off the porch and down to his truck. Melvin quickly followed.

"What are you doin'? Huh?"

"Señor Malveen, I can no longer work for choo, just pay me what choo owe me and choo can keep dee brushes. Se frecuenta este lugar, this place is haunted! "

Melvin stood tall. He placed his hands on Mr. Carlos's shoulders and looked him in the eye. He spoke very calmly to him.

"Look Mr. C. I'm sure there's some logical explanation for this. Now come on, come on now let's talk about this."

"BULLSHIT! That's what it is," came a yell from the top of the stairs. There was Dave standing in the doorway, holding a hot cup of coffee, tilting a bottle of rum over the cup and pouring just enough to complete his mixture.

"Yep, that's right. It's bullshit glue you're usin'."

Mr. Carlos snatched himself out of the hands of Melvin and climbed in his truck.

"There's notting wrong with my paint or dee glue! Choo can send me a check Señor Malveen. Sorry."

He pulled away looking back at the house. As he drove down the driveway, they could still hear him yelling, "Se frecuenta este lugar!"

At the opposite side of the yard, a voice screamed out, "Melvin, hey Melvin, it's me, Marie. Is Mr. Carlos angry at you? Why you just send him right on over here and I'll calm Poppy down. How are you feeling? Are you tense, too? I know exactly what you need, you hot chocolate stud. You think I can borrow some of that hot black meat tonight neighbor?"

Melvin looked up the stairs at Dave and shook his head.

"You know, she's really startin' to irritate the hell out of me."

"Wait Melvin," Dave started to grin. He peered at Marie at the fence. "Maybe the ho can paint!"

Dave started laughing and walked over and sat on the banister. He sat there and watched Marie, as she stood there licking one of the bars of the fence and fondling herself.

"You know, if you fixed her hair, put some nice clothes on her, a little perfume, replaced her tits, legs, and ass, and chopped her head off, she wouldn't be half bad."

Dave took another sip of the liquid in his cup. He and Marie exchanged obscenities. After a few minutes, Melvin couldn't take anymore.

"Man bring your ass on, and leave that crazy broad alone," Melvin's voice rang from the darkness.

He sat Dave down and tried explaining what had happened with the room. Of course, Dave laughed.

CHAPTER 11   THE VISIT

The last remains of the golden colored Jamaican rum had just been poured into the glass. Melvin pulled himself up off the couch and made his way into the kitchen. Pressing his glass gently against the ice dispenser, he allowed only two cubes of ice to fall into the glass. He walked to the front door and looked out at the vacant driveway. He had forgotten that Dave had driven his car home and was bringing it back in the morning. He closed and locked the front door and flopped back down on the couch.

He grabbed the remote control from the coffee table and began channel surfing while still enjoying his beverage. He finally stopped on the Sci-fi channel and became mesmerized by an old re-run of a Star Trek episode. He loved Star Trek, and the Sci-Fi channel was running an all night marathon.

Melvin settled himself in and propped his feet up on the armrest of the couch. He continued to watch Captain Kirk zap the aliens and kiss green women until he drifted off to sleep. Periodically, he would dream of aliens chasing him or that he was flying the Starship Enterprise. He was really enjoying his dream-scape. He lay in a deep rest and was having a wonderful dream.

This particular dream felt so real to him. It was about a beautiful alien woman with a really nice firm round ass and she had three nice breasts. She found him lying by a rock, half naked, weak and wounded. She tried squirting alien milk from her breast in his mouth and over his face to bring him back to conscious-ness, but it did no good. She then realized that the only thing that could possibly energize him would be to give him oral sex. Of course, her lips were full and juicy. Her tongue was long and wet. After all, it was HIS dream. Just as she was about to go down on him, Captain Kirk beamed down beside her.

He had Doctor Spock put a lock on Melvin and the alien woman and set new coordinates for the two to be beamed up to the Starship Enterprise. Instead, they were beamed to a cold planet in a faraway galaxy. It was freezing there and Melvin still couldn't wake up. Still trying to save him, the alien woman kneeled next to Melvin. She rubbed his cold meat until it was hot and hard. He managed to open his eyes some, but was still too weak to move. Melvin watched her as she slid down his pants and placed his member to her mouth. She was caressing and licking it so good. Then she placed it in her mouth and started sucking and licking as if she was doing it for her survival. He could feel her alien claws scratching into the side of his thigh while she did this. He didn't mind though, because he was still enjoying the best oral satisfaction that he had ever had. She kept sucking and licking until he could do nothing else but explode. After she had let all that he had into her mouth and onto her warm tongue, she gently pulled up his trousers.

Just as the sun began to make its way through the glass of the front door window, Melvin tried opening his eyes. He closed them again and began to rub them to clear up the dry residue that had embedded itself in the small openings during the night. He reached up and grabbed the back of the couch and pulled himself up to a sitting position. He stomped his feet and rubbed his legs in hopes of getting the blood circulating back through them after having them propped up all night. He stood up and stretched his arms outward while looking around the room. He didn't remember turning off the television, and he also noticed dampness on the walls.

Melvin made his way up the steps and down the hall to the master bedroom. He went straight through to the master bathroom. He turned on the shower and walked back into his room where he sat on the edge of the bed listening to the shower water running and thinking of the sex dream that he had last night. As he pulled off his pants and underwear he was sure to find the stain from his ejaculation. He held his underpants up towards the ceiling to check for the dried stain, but there was no stain. They were not soiled at all.

"Man, what a dream. I even felt like I had busted a wad. Whoa!"

Melvin stripped naked and stepped into the shower. He grabbed the soap from the holder and started lathering up his body. "What the hell?"

Melvin felt pain on his thigh. He looked down to see what was causing the burning sensation on his upper thigh. As he leaned over to get a closer look, he noticed there were four long scratches running up his leg.

"Where in the hell did that come from?" he thought.

He remembered eating his chicken burrito. He remembered walking Dave out, having a couple of drinks, and watching Star Trek, but nothing that would have caused the scratches. He finished washing the rest of his body, but avoided that area. He got out of the shower, dried off and got dressed. Downstairs, Mel poured himself a cup of coffee and again tried to revisit his actions the night before. Then it hit him, the dream. He remembered the alien scratching his leg with her claws during their oral encounter. He took another sip of the coffee.

"BAM! BAM! BAM!" The knocks were so hard, the front door rattled with each one. Melvin got up and walked over to the door and opened it.

There stood Dave holding a box of white powdered Hostess donuts and presenting his early morning grin.

"The bitch has a key to my place!" Melvin said as he grabbed the doorknob and started checking the locks.

"What are you talkin' 'bout? What bitch?" Dave asked.

Melvin poked his head out the door as Dave stepped in. He examined the front door again then shut it.

"The ho next door. I think she was in here last night."

Dave turned and looked at Melvin.

"Why do you say that man? Is something missing? Did you see or hear her in here?"

Melvin's face was beginning to turn beet red. He started scratching his face and head. He walked over and sat down in his big fluffy corner chair.

"Nah, I just know she was in here that's all."

"How?" Dave asked again.

"Well somebody was here, but I know it was her."

Dave walked over and sat on the couch. He pulled out one of the white dusty donuts and extended the box toward Melvin. Melvin waved his hand to decline. Dave leaned back and placed his left leg on top of the coffee table.

"You gonna tell me what in the hell happened man? You aint makin' no sense. No sense at all man."

Melvin folded his arms and looked down at the floor.

"Well yeah, somethin' did happen. Somebody was in here last night while I was asleep. They did somethin' to me. I still think it was Marie, too."

"What'd they do? Or should I say, what'd she do to make you think she was here?"

Melvin started scratching his head again. He turned his head and looked out of the window. He told Dave about his dream. He told him about the alien woman finding him by the rock. He told him about the alien oral sex and how she had scratched him. Then he looked back down at the floor. Dave had finished his donut and had just reached in the box for another. "You got any coffee?" Dave mumbled.

Melvin jumped out of his chair and looked down at Dave.

"Man I'm serious! The scratches are there. The ho got in here some kind of way and the ho blew me! I'm tellin' you, she ran outta here with a mouth full of my juices!"

"Okay, alright! I can see why you're pissed. Now let's just say that this is true. That only means that you either got a blow-job from your crazy ass, nasty lookin', tar and nicotine ingested, dysentery carryin' neighbor or a sack suckin' alien slut from the planet Ballickium. Come on man, it was just a dream, but I know what you mean. On the real, I'd rather walk through a lion's cage with a double-breasted pork chop suit on before I'd let that skank next door blow me. Let's face it man, you had a lot to drink last night and you probably just scratched yourself in your sleep tryin' to get to those little balls of yours."

Melvin unbuttoned his pants and pulled both his pants and underwear down to his knees displaying the deep scratches.

"Just a dream huh? Whatever!"

Dave jumped up and started laughing.

"Damn man, I'm tryin' to eat here. Come on man, put that thing away before you put somebody's eye out. You could have poked me in the eye right through the hole in my donut. I'm sure it would have fit, too and with room to spare."

Dave was now laughing like a mad man. Melvin pulled his pants back up and stormed off toward the kitchen.

"Looks like that alien chick would have had to come from the planet Littlepricksuckus with lips like a goldfish to have those kinds of skills you described. See, that ho would have died from lockjaw tryin' to wrap those tiny lips around this python. Hey, can you send her over to my place tonight? She can scratch me all she wants as long as she makes a withdrawal. By the way, is that a damn thong you're wearin'?"

"Damn right! Hey man, support in front with ass freedom in the back. Hey look man, with an ass this size, your drawls gone cram up in your ass anyway, so what the hell."

"You are one nasty, freaky individual Mel. No wonder alien hos are tryin' to get a piece."

Dave giggled for a while by himself. Neither man spoke another word about the incident the rest of the day.

CHAPTER 12   THE NEXT VISIT

That evening, Melvin and Dave sat out on the porch having what they liked to call an "open air happy hour".

"I'd better call a cab man. I've been socializing with your ass long enough for one day."

Melvin turned the beer can up to his mouth and downed the rest of the contents. He slid the can under his foot and stepped down on it until it was completely flattened.

"You can take the car if you want. You comin' by here tomorrow?"

Dave stood up to stretch his tired body after a long day of doing nothing.

"Don't know. You know, I've got that thing to do tomorrow and you know I've got that speakin' engagement at the White House with Bush, oh yeah, and I do have to go and present my cure for cancer over at Johns Hopkins."

"Man, shut the hell up," Melvin yelled out while laughing.

Dave started laughing then turned up his can and gulped down the rest of his beer.

"Yeah, I gotta stop through tomorrow. I gotta hear what happens to you tonight. Maybe a werewolf or a vampire will break in and violate your body next. I hear werewolves love the booty, so you'd better sleep on your back and in some tight drawls tonight dude."

Melvin stood up and just pointed his finger at Dave. He walked into the house and came back out with his car keys in his hand. Dave had sat back down on the step, now rubbing his head.

"You sure you can drive man? I mean, you look like shit."

"Wow, how many beers did I have?"

Melvin placed the keys in his pant pocket.

"I could do both of you tonight, that's how horny I am. Suck you both dry," shouted the voice from the fence.

It was none other than Marie. This time she was standing by the fence smoking a cigarette in her robe and slippers, with a Washington Redskins baseball cap on her head and powdered blue gloves on her hands.

"Who over there wants to fuck? Huh? This'll be the best pussy you'll ever have in your life. Are you guys queer or what? If so, who wants to get 'turned out' as you say?"

Melvin placed his foot on the step below where Dave was sitting. He put his hand under Dave's armpit and helped him up. As they turned toward the house, they could still hear Marie in the background.

"Fuckin' queers! Ok, you don't have to fuck me, just let me sit on somebody's face. C'mon! Give me one of those mustache rides! Oh shit, I just came! See what you did?! You got me all soggy, Baby. Nobody has ever made me feel this good. Well, not since your uncle died, anyway. C'mon! I already love you!"

Both men walked into the house and Melvin slammed the door behind them.

Melvin could hear the sawing of trees, and the sounds of cheap metal roller skates, scratching across the concrete pavement echoing through the upstairs hallway. At least that's what it sounded like.

Dave's snoring from the downstairs couch was so loud that it kept Melvin awake for hours. He lay in his bed listening for a key to turn in his front door so that he could catch Marie red handed. He made a mental note to himself to check into getting a security system.

He switched the button on the side of his radio on the nightstand to the "on" position. Then he pressed the preset button on his radio to 96.3 "WHUR." After realizing that Marie was not going to make an appearance, he snuggled down in his bed. Listening to the smooth calm music of the "Quiet Storm," Melvin dozed off to sleep. He wasn't in the same deep sleep as the night before. He would slip in and out of consciousness. At times, he could still hear Dave sawing down those trees in the near distance.

Half asleep, he suddenly felt very cold. It was the kind of cold that made your bones ache. It was the same cold that he felt on the planet that Captain Kirk had him beamed to. He reached down and pulled the covers over his head and tried to ignore it. He was able to drift back off to sleep. After about an hour, Melvin was awakened again by the same familiar feeling that he had experienced the night before. He felt the warmth of her mouth taking him inside. His first reaction was to jump up and grab Marie by her hair and drag her out of his house, but it was feeling so good. Good enough not to make her stop.

He listened for the snoring sounds from downstairs. Dave was still at it. That was all he needed. He had decided to let her finish before he confronted her. His legs were beginning to shake and then it hit. He had shot another hot load of his insides. As his volcanic eruption took place, he sat up quickly in his bed pretending to be shocked by her presence. She was not there. There wasn't another soul in sight.

The covers were pulled back below his knees, his penis was poking through the slot of his underwear and his warm body fluids were disappearing into thin air.

"What the fu...?"

Melvin jumped out of his bed and started to run out of his room. With his sweatpants now down to his ankles, Melvin fell hard against the bedroom wall. It was damp and clammy feeling, the same as the night before. He picked himself up and headed down the hall calling out to Dave.

E.L. RHODES

When Melvin reached the bottom step, he found Dave sprawled out over the couch in the living room. His right leg was thrown over the back of the couch and his left was draped over the corner of the coffee table. He had one hand buried in his crotch and sucking the thumb of the other.

"Dave! Wake the hell up man!" Mel yelled at the top of his lungs.

Melvin took his hand and pushed Dave's leg off the coffee table.

"Get up man!"

Dave slowly pulled his thumb out from his mouth and then the other hand from its resting place.

"What's up Mel? What in the hell are you yellin' about this early in the mornin'?"

Melvin walked over and looked up the stairs leading to the hall. He could smell the stench from where he had defecated in his underwear from being scared out of his wits. He walked back over to Dave and pointed to the stairway. "It happened again man. I'm tellin' you, and I'm not trippin' either."

Dave sat up on the couch. He extended his hand out to Melvin, because he was in need of some assistance in order to stand up.

"You must be out of your damn mind if you think I'm tou-chin' that dick beater. Man you been cuppin' your nuts all night with that hand, you better get your own ass up!"

Dave wiped his hand on his sweatpants then placed it up to his nose and took a sniff, "Ahhhhh, there's nothin' like the fresh scent of balls to get your mornin' started," he mumbled with a grin on his face.

Melvin was too busy concentrating on the upstairs to pay him any attention. Dave managed to lift himself to his feet. He walked over to where Melvin stood and looked up the steps at the vacant hallway.

"Uh, what are we lookin' at, and what in the hell is that foul smell?"

Melvin headed up the steps and motioned for Dave to follow. The men entered the room. Melvin looked around then walked over and slid his hand up and down the wall near the door. The room was no longer cold. The walls were no longer clammy, but you could still smell the dampness in the air.

"Again, what are we lookin' for man? You woke me up to see your junky ass room? AND WHAT IS THAT DAMN SMELL? It smells like shit in here!"

Dave now standing in the doorway scratching his crotch was ready to return to his resting place. Melvin dropped to his knees and looked under the bed. He pulled out a few socks, a box of receipts, and a plastic container filled with old videos then rose to his feet. He looked at Dave quizzically then sat on the side of the bed.

"I don't get it. Man, I could have sworn that I was layin' here and somebody was in here toppin' me off again. I thought it was Marie, but that old ho can't possibly run that fast. I jumped up and nobody was there. It was freezin' in here, too. I know I wasn't dreamin'."

"Sheeeit, well don't look at me man. We close bro, but we aint that damn close!" Dave turned, stuck his head out and looked down both ends of the hallway. "Man, you need to stop smokin' and drinkin'. That's all there is to it. You sure you don't have some sick thing for that old critter next door? That's sick and nasty, but if you do, I'll understand. I'll tell everybody that we know, but I'll understand."

Dave stepped into the hall then turned and looked at Melvin. "C'mon man, let's eat. I'm cookin'. You gotta be hungry seein' that you just got blown and all! Smells like she blew the shit out of you, too! I'm hungry. We'll eat and then I'm goin' back to bed and maybe I'll get a blow job, too."

Melvin didn't laugh. He just got up and went into the bathroom and cleaned himself up. He slipped his sweatpants back on and then followed Dave downstairs. He stopped on the stairway and looked back at the room then yelled out to Dave, "Yeah, just make sure you wash those night nut holders of yours before you cook anythin' that I'm gonna eat."

Dave reached down and grabbed his crotch.

"You sure you don't need to add a little salt to your diet? You know sweaty sack salt has less sodium than regular salt."

They chuckled as they made their way to the kitchen. Dave pulled out a couple of pans and laid them on the stove. He walked over to the refrigerator and opened it.

"Hands man, wash those nasty hands before you go diggin' in my fridge."

Dave looked back at Melvin smiling. He slammed the door to the refrigerator and proceeded to wash his hands in the kitchen sink. Afterwards, he dried his hands with the towel that was stuffed between the handle of the oven door. He walked towards Melvin with his hands extended.

"Satisfied, Dad? I just lowered your blood pressure by ten points."

Dave returned to the refrigerator and started pulling out everything that he needed for their meal preparation. He tossed six strips of bacon in the large frying pan and was now cracking some eggs. Then off in the distance, they heard a familiar sound, a distinct sound which made them both laugh.

"What the hell? It's four thirty in the mornin'. What's he doin' out this time of night? Was that comin' from next door? I don't believe it. He really is tappin' 'Naszilla'. Maybe she had an emergency. She probably had a busted water pipe or an electrical problem or somethin'. He just didn't sneak over there to hit that. I'm sure we're just jumpin' to conclusions. If he's hittin' that, I'm sure she's payin' him, 'cause you know Mr. C. is all about makin' a buck."

Dave looked at Melvin shaking his head and looking disgusted. They heard Mr. Carlos' pickup making its usual clicking and back firing down Marie's driveway.

"But you've got to draw the line somewhere. Some people's hypocrisy has no bounds! That's your boy."

"I guess he's just tryin' to feed his family. You know he's got a rack of kids; there's at least eight of 'em I think and I think his wife is pregnant again."

"Well it sounds like your boy just likes to fuck! Eight, nine kids, now that's some fuckin'. Nah, he aint tryin' to feed his kids... He's tryin' to feed his dick! And you know that lizard licker next door is givin' him all that he can handle. My kids would be livin' off fried rat ass and pigeon beaks before I'd stoop that damn low."

Dave pulled a fork out of the drawer next to the stove. He jabbed it into each piece of bacon and flipped them over one at a time. Melvin, still giggling and shaking his head in disbelief, started making coffee. After the bacon was under control, Dave turned and leaned on the sink before continuing.

"Damn man, I need to get back to the city. It's just too much alien shit goin' on out here. I mean, you've got space aliens givin' blowjobs. You've got illegal aliens fuckin' nasty aliens from the planet "Next Door". It's just too much for me. Look at me man, I'm a wreck. I still can't stop my eye from twitchin'."

Dave went back to the meal. He pulled out the pieces of bacon and placed them neatly on the paper towel that was draped over a plate. He dumped the bowl of eggs into the pan and started stirring them. Melvin poured the hot black liquid into two large mugs and placed them on the counter. Dave looked at the mug that Melvin had placed near him.

"Man, I aint drinkin' that. What, you think I'm stayin' up with your scary ass, oh hell no! I'm eatin' and then I'm takin' my ass back to sleep. You still thinkin' about aliens and Marie, and vanishin' cum shots aren't you? I tell you what, if the alien comes back to top you off, let it and then shoot it. If Marie sneaks in here and tops you off, shoot her, too. Better yet, let me shoot her ass. And if your cum is disappearin' again, you've already shot off so who cares? Just go back to sleep. You see, problem solved. Food's ready!"

Melvin said nothing. He knew that Dave didn't fully know or understand what was happening but he knew that he wasn't crazy. The men ate and returned back to bed. Laying there wide awake, Melvin couldn't stop thinking about what had happened earlier. He questioned his sanity. He kept visualizing his ejaculated stream vanishing right before his eyes; he tried over and over to justify what he saw. He tried to rationalize, but he just couldn't.

"Maybe Marie really is an alien. Maybe she can disappear or travel at the speed of light or somethin'. She was pretty good though, and if I never have to see her… what am I thinkin'? This is crazy. I was probably still asleep. Maybe Dave is right. Maybe I should stop drinkin'."

Suddenly, the room started getting cold again. Melvin reached down and pulled the covers up to his neck. He turned over onto his side, pulled his knees up closer to his body and folded his arms.

The room was still freezing. Melvin quickly jumped out of bed and slipped his feet into his slippers. As he walked down the upstairs hall he could feel the cold air surrounding him. He walked downstairs into the living room where he saw Dave laying on the couch with his hand tucked back into its salty resting place. He made his way over to the thermostat at which time the cold air stopped immediately. It was warm again.

Dave was now snoring louder than ever. Melvin shrugged his shoulders and went back upstairs. He went into every room and checked the windows, every room, except the pink one. There was something about that room that was very unsettling to Melvin.

He pushed the door open slowly. He peered in. He felt strange. He could feel something unnatural; a presence of some kind. He couldn't quite explain it to himself. He backed away from the room and headed back down the hall. He still felt uneasy.

As he approached the entrance to his bedroom, Melvin looked back down the hall at the room. He stopped dead in his tracks. The door to the room was now closed.

"That must be where the cold air is comin' from. I'll check it in the mornin'. Yeah, I'll check it when Dave gets up."

Melvin climbed back in his bed and lay awake thinking for the rest of the night.

CHAPTER 13   THE DATE

That morning Melvin still did not return to the room. He saw that the door was still closed and left it that way. The day had passed. The guys had done their normal routine, nothing. They played video games, went to the mall, and down to The Sapphire to touch on the weekly current events.

On the way back home, Melvin dropped Dave off at his house. This was a big night for Melvin. He was going out with Wendy tonight. He had finally made it happen. He and Wendy had kept in contact since the day she had stopped by his old apartment. She would call him on his cell phone from work almost every day.

Melvin knew deep down, maybe not so deep, hell, he knew what she was really after, but he still could not resist her. She was still the woman of his dreams. He didn't care that all she was really looking for was a free ride or a little spending cash here and there. To have her on his arm is all that he ever wanted. Well the sex, too, I guess I shouldn't leave that out.

Melvin went home and cleaned up the house. He put a nice bottle of wine in the fridge along with the cheese tray that he had bought for the occasion. He had the entire night planned down to the second. First, an early dinner, then a movie and then back to the house for some butt naked twister.

During his cleaning, Melvin went up to his room and made up the bed. He tossed all of the dirty socks in the laundry basket and swept the floor. He had just gone into the bathroom to retrieve the dirty clothes from the hamper to wash them when it hit him.

"Damn! What in the hell is that smell?"

Melvin lifted the top of the hamper cover and the smell from hell poured out. He sifted through the laundry until he came across the pair of underwear that he had soiled that morning. He lifted them up only to see a skid mark as wide as a snickers bar running from mid butt crack down to his scrotum edge. Melvin pinched the underwear between his forefinger and thumb and quickly took them downstairs. He placed them in a white plastic trash bag and threw them in the outside trash bin. After which he went back upstairs and collected the remaining clothing for the laundry.

The house was ready. The wine was chilling, and the bubble bath was next to the tub. Melvin took a shower, put on his clothes and headed out to the car.

"You look good Baby. You look so good I could just eat you up. Come and get some. You know you want it!"

Marie was yelling from the fence as Melvin climbed into the car. Melvin flipped his middle finger in her direction and slid onto the car seat.

"I can drain a couple of ounces from you. Make you look lighter and clear your skin up, too! C'mon, it'll relax you for your big date," she continued.

Melvin pulled off and headed for Wendy's. As he drove past the fence, he could see Marie raising her tee shirt and displaying her braless breasts. After catching a glimpse of the two saggy puppy ears, he sped off without looking back. As he turned from his driveway, he passed Mr. Carlos in his pickup clicking and sputtering. Melvin slowed down and looked into his rearview mirror as he watched Mr. Carlos' pickup pull into Marie's driveway.

"Damn! Guess I'm not the only one gettin' lucky tonight," Melvin shouted. He laughed and continued to Wendy's.

It was a plain looking building. It was definitely not what Melvin had expected. He parked the car and made his way up the courtyard. "4802" was posted on the side of the building. Melvin went inside and took the steps two at a time. He stopped in front of the door. Apartment number four is where she lived. Melvin stood there for a second. He adjusted his clothes and slid the tops of both shoes down the back of each pant leg for a quick, last minute buff. He tapped on the door and waited quietly. He was so nervous that he had to remind himself to breathe.

The door opened and there stood Wendy. She was looking as sexy as ever. After seeing her, all of his nervousness packed up and left.

"Look at you standing there like you're just waiting to get all sopped up!" Melvin whispered while shaking his head. This was his attempt at being sexy. He figured the old lady from the old job was on to something. That fake suave approach worked on the young lady at The Sapphire, so he might as well give it a shot on Wendy.

"You look great woman. You ready to go?"

Wendy walked over and pulled her trench coat out of the closet and then reached over and picked up her keys off the end table.

"Ready," she said displaying a forced smile.

They walked down to the car. Melvin opened the door for Wendy and she climbed into the passenger seat. Melvin jumped into the car, looked at Wendy and smiled. He still couldn't believe it. He was actually taking Wendy out.

He turned the key in the ignition and the music blasted throughout the automobile. Melvin wasn't used to having a nice stereo, so he blasted everything every chance he got. He pressed the button for the CD player and selected CD number "4". Once the music started, he snapped on his seat belt and slowly pulled out into traffic.

"So what are we doing tonight?" Wendy asked.

"Well, I thought we'd head up to Georgetown and have dinner, then check out a movie or some music. We could go to the club, any club. What clubs do you like? We can do whatever you want. Dinner and a movie, you cool with that?"

Wendy reached down and turned the volume button of the radio. She turned the music down to a whisper. She looked over at Melvin and then placed her hand gently on his arm.

"I'm not really that hungry and I really don't want to waste a lot of time sitting in a movie theater. Do you have something at your place that we could snack on, and maybe a DVD?"

Melvin knew this was her way of trying to avoid being seen with him by any of her co-workers or friends. He also knew that this would not be just his "do or die" night, but hers as well. He knew what she wanted, but just how far would she be willing to go? He had decided that he was pulling out all the stops. Melvin headed for the bridge.

As they rode along, Melvin reached over and turned the radio back up. He placed his hand on her thigh and asked if she was sure that she wanted to go straight to his place. She confirmed her position and he continued on.

Melvin pulled up to the front of the house. He climbed out of the car and walked around to open Wendy's door. Before he had gotten there, she had opened her door and started to climb out. "This is really nice Melvin."

She slid her long legs out of the car and Melvin offered her his hand to help her out of the seat. It was faint at first, but then it became very loud and very annoying very quickly.

"I said, WHO THE FUCK IS THAT?!"

Marie was now yanking on the bars of the fence and kicking up dust. Melvin and Wendy looked over at the frail figure acting like an angry caged monkey.

"Nobody fucks my man, NOBODY! So don't get any fuckin' ideas!" she continued.

Wendy looked at Melvin strangely.

"What have you been doing out here Melvin? Have you been…?"

Before she could finish her statement, Melvin jumped in to defend himself. He couldn't let Wendy think for one second that he had been sleeping with Marie, even though he still wasn't quite sure about a blow job or two.

"Aw, don't pay that old crazy wind bag no mind. She's crazy!"

"You're gonna pay for this Melvin, you're gonna pay! C'mon Baby, don't do this to me. You love me. Don't you still love me? Besides, this is the only pussy for you. Only this one! Come feel it, come taste it. Come smell it! I smell it all the time; taste it too. It tastes good Melvin, real good. NOW GET THE FUCK AWAY FROM MY MAN, BITCH!!" Marie continued.

"Oh wait, I know that hag didn't just call me a bitch?" Wendy exclaimed while snatching off her earrings and snatching her coat off.

"Nah Baby, I told you she's just crazy. I hear she was just released from Saint Elizabeth's. Shut up woman! Wit your crazy ass, and get away from my property!" Melvin finally yelled back.

Melvin placed his hand behind Wendy's arm and escorted her up the stairs. Marie continued yelling her obscenities until they had reached the top of the stairs and out of her sight. Melvin unlocked the door and opened it slowly. He stepped aside and Wendy walked in.

"Wow Melvin, you really have a nice place with the exception of your girlfriend next door. That bitch IS crazy! How do you put up with that mess? Anyway, enough of that. Now, how have you been? I've really missed you not being at work. I especially miss you coming up there in the morning talking all that trash. You know I was never actually mad at you, don't you? I was just giving you a hard time. Playing hard to get, you know?"

Melvin said nothing. He walked over to the coffee table and picked up the remote control to the stereo and clicked it on.

"I've got some wine and cheese in the fridge. Want some?"

Wendy sat down and looked over at Melvin. She smiled and then pulled the edge of her skirt over her knee.

"Yeah, that would be nice."

Melvin headed for the kitchen smiling. He fumbled around in the kitchen for a minute, and then returned with the tray and the bottle of white zinfandel wine.

"Why don't you let me slip those shoes off for you?"

He dropped to one knee and held out his hand. Wendy stuck one foot out, then the other. Melvin slipped off both of her shoes and placed them neatly under the coffee table. He noticed that her feet stank of old pepperoni and bleu cheese but he could overlook her one little flaw.

"Damn, suddenly I've got a taste for pizza. You sure you're not hungry?" Melvin asked while still inhaling her shoe scent.

He poured them both a glass of wine and they listened to music and talked for about a half hour or so. Melvin picked up the bottle and began pouring more of the light colored liquid into Wendy's glass.

"Why Melvin Dossier, you're trying to get me drunk aren't you?"

Melvin just smiled and continued pouring. Melvin then slid closer to Wendy. She took a huge gulp from her glass then stuck it out for a refill. Melvin reached back and grabbed the bottle. He emptied the remaining contents into her glass. He sat the empty bottle on the table and continued his advancement.

Melvin placed his hand behind Wendy's head and slowly began to pull her face in his direction. Now a little tipsy, she was still not ready to deal with this reality. She closed her eyes and pictured Denzel Washington in her mind, but could still see fragments of Melvin through the cracks of her eyelids.

"Can we make it a little darker in here?" She asked as she withdrew.

Melvin looked at her. He knew what she was trying to do but he didn't care. He climbed up off the couch and strut his pointy tee pee over to the dimmer knob on the wall. He turned the knob counter clockwise and the room darkened.

"How's that?"

Wendy looked around the room then answered, "Darker, please."

Melvin continued to turn the knob and repeatedly asked for Wendy's approval. It wasn't until the room was completely dark that she was satisfied. Melvin sat back down and started to kiss her again.

"Can the room get any darker?"

Melvin let out a deep sigh. He gently slid his hand over her eyelids and moved in closer. Denzel's image returned and was now working. She held on tight to that image in her mind and let go. Melvin placed his lips on Wendy's then slowly entered her mouth with his tongue. She welcomed it. Melvin was starting to sweat just from the thought of being on his way to the score of his life. Then it hit. Wendy pushed Melvin back off of her.

"What in the hell is that smell Melvin? Tell me that's not your breath."

Melvin sat up and cupped his hands together. He blew into his hands and sniffed. "Girl you trippin', I don't smell noth..."

Just as he began to speak, the stench rushed up his nose and into his mouth. He could actually taste it.

"Woman, did you bust your ass? Damn, that stinks!"

Melvin jumped up and rushed back over to the dimmer. He snatched it back around and the room illuminated. They both started sniffing around the area. Melvin got up to check the refrigerator for rotted food. Wendy sat up and sniffed around her body. The smell seemed to be coming from her or her clothing.

While Melvin was still in the kitchen checking out the refrigerator, Wendy smelled every piece of clothing that she was wearing. She leaned over and picked up one of her shoes and inhaled the entire inside. She smelled the pepperoni, but it wasn't the stench that they were looking for. She checked out her armpits and then between her legs. That's when she smelled the horrific stench the strongest.

She sat forward and turned toward the back of the couch and took a deep breath. It was coming from the couch. Not being sure if it was coming from behind or inside, she sniffed between the cushions and the back of the couch. She sat up and peered through the crack of the cushion on which she was currently sitting. She now knew where the smell was coming from. She stood up and lifted the cushion from the couch.

She walked over to the fireplace and grabbed a poker from the rack and stuck it into the opening of the cloth and lifted. It was a pair of soiled underpants. Actually, it was the same pair that Melvin had on earlier that morning. It was the exact pair that he had his accident in.

Melvin walked back into the room. Wendy was holding the garment up by the poker. Melvin could see the huge skid mark as he approached.

"What in the hell is this Melvin? Are these yours, and if so, have you ever heard of toilet paper? Damn!"

Melvin just stood there with the most shocked and embarrassed look on his face. Wendy lowered the garment and ran for the bathroom. Melvin could hear her vomiting from the living room. It was truly disgusting. Not quite the evening he had planned.

Wendy returned from the bathroom looking at Melvin as if he was the nastiest human being on this earth; no make that in the universe.

"I don't know where those came from. Surely you don't believe that those are mine? They were probably there when I bought this couch," Melvin explained.

Wendy said nothing. She just sat staring out of the window, still holding her stomach. Finally she looked over at Melvin. What she said to him then, he would remember for the rest of his life. "Take me home."

Melvin's explaining now kicked into overdrive. "Look here, I told you they're not mine. C'mon don't mess up a nice night."

Wendy stood up and walked over to the chair where her coat and purse rested. She picked up her purse and reached inside and retrieved her cell phone. "You messed up this night the second you shitted in those drawls, Melvin."

Wendy flipped open her phone and stepped out onto the porch. After about five minutes, she returned and sat down on the chair across from Melvin.

"Why are you trippin' like this baby?"

Wendy just sat still in the chair. She said nothing. Melvin sat there quietly as well, trying to figure out how in the hell those underwear made it back into the house. He could hear a car in the distance now getting closer.

The brakes made a squealing sound as the car came to a dead stop in front of the house. Two short blasts from the horn came from the vehicle.

"That's my cab. I have to go Melvin. I'll call you tomorrow, okay?"

Melvin sat there still puzzled and pissed.

"Don't bother," he mumbled.

Wendy looked back at him and then walked out the door, closing it behind her.

"Damn honey that was quick. I told you that this is the only one for him. Maybe you should let a real woman come over and satisfy him right! I'll make him squeal like a pig!" yelled the voice from the fence.

After hearing the car door slam shut and the car pull off, Melvin rose to his feet and watched the woman of his dreams ride out of his life. He knew she could never get past that. Melvin went to the couch and sat down. He kept thinking about the underwear and how they could have possibly have gotten there. No one could have possibly been there while he was out, no one except Dave.

"Dave, that bastard!" he thought. Melvin dug down into his pocket and pulled out his cell phone. He punched in Dave's number and placed the phone to his ear. While waiting for Dave to answer, he walked into the kitchen and pulled out the second bottle of wine that he had purchased to assist in his conquest. After several rings the voice on the other end of the phone finally answered. "Yeah?"

"You bastard, how could you do this to me? That wasn't funny man, not at all. Wendy got sick, pissed, frightened and then went home. My only question is why?"

Melvin rested the phone between the side of his face and his left shoulder. He sat the wine bottle on the counter top in the kitchen and inserted the metal corkscrew. Pausing between twists, he listened to the voice coming from the phone.

"Man, what in the hell are you talking about? And why what?" said the voice.

"You came by here right? You set me up? You know what I'm talkin' 'bout, the couch thing."

Melvin continued twisting the plastic handle of the corkscrew clockwise then stopped.

"Mel, I haven't been back over there man. I have no damn idea what in the hell you're talkin' about. After you dropped me off, I rode with Nate and Teddy up the road. We're just gettin' back."

Melvin pulled the cork from the bottle. He could hear both Nate and Teddy in the background talking. He knew that Dave would have never brought them to his house and could tell that he wasn't lying. He knew him too well.

"Damn, if not you, then who? Somebody was in here."

Melvin turned the bottle up to his lips and took several gulps. The voice spoke from the phone again. "What happened man?"

Melvin told Dave what happened. He didn't mention the underwear; he just said that it was something that he had placed in the trash outside. A garment which he had spilled food on and produced a terrible odor. Dave started to laugh. Melvin placed the bottle on the counter and sat down on one of the bar stools.

"See, there you go again man, everything is a joke."

Dave continued to laugh until it faded.

"Nah man, it just sounds pretty stupid to me, and you expected me to believe that? You know, that is almost as stupid as the time when we were kids and you had a bunch of us all sad and shit because you told us that your goldfish had drowned. Now what kind of monkey shit is that? A damn fish drownin'? And you even had Sandie walkin' around the neighborhood takin' up a collection for his funeral. C'mon man, I aint buyin' this no more than I bought that goldfish story.

So you're sayin' she went crazy over a shirt with garlic and tomato sauce? No way! If that's the case, she's crazy, too. I'll catch you in the a.m. man, got some things to handle."

Melvin collapsed his cell phone and placed it back into his pocket. He walked outside and checked the trashcan, but there was no sign of a second white trash bag containing soiled underpants. He returned inside still puzzled.

He walked back over to the counter, picked up the bottle of wine. He went back into the living room and flopped down on the couch. He tried calling Wendy several times to try to explain again, but she would not answer. After leaving her a third message, he tossed his phone on the coffee table and leaned back.

CHAPTER 14   BACK AGAIN

Melvin sat there sipping the wine and trying to come up with some reasonable explanation for the underwear, but couldn't. After emptying the entire contents of the bottle, he picked his cell phone from off of the coffee table and decided to try Wendy once more.

The phone rang over and over then her sweet voice would answer directing the caller to leave a message. Melvin tossed the phone back on the table. He laid back and rested his head on the back of the couch.

With his head spinning, he fell into a deep sleep. He wanted to forget about that night. He dreamed of how it could have been. He could see her lying naked beside him. He could even feel her lips on his and her tongue swimming inside his mouth. Her hand was rubbing between his legs and had him aroused. "I'm dreamin'. I know I'm dreamin'."

Melvin fought his way back into consciousness and opened his eyes slightly. It was freezing again in the room. Still squinting, he was about to get up to check the thermostat when he realized that he could still feel Wendy's soft thick lips kissing him and caressing his throbbing flesh. Melvin froze. He couldn't move. He realized that he was actually awake and was actually with someone in the room. He mustered up enough courage to open his eyes completely and everything stopped. He sat up quickly.

He saw the curtains move then the picture on the wall leading up the stairs shift to the right. It was as if someone had brushed against it. Melvin was petrified. He pulled his knees up to his chest and did not move. He sat in the same spot with his eyes wide open and shaking for the rest of the night. He was afraid. He sat rocking until morning.

The next morning as usual, a loud knock came at the door. Melvin did not move. The next successions of knocks were louder than the first.

"Mel, you in there?"

Then he could hear the voice shouting in another direction.

"Take your little nasty ass back in the house you old slut. It's too early in the mornin' to be listenin' to your shit. Mel, open up! It's me."

Mel did not move or speak.

"Yo man! Open up!" yelled the voice.

Melvin looked around the room and slowly slid himself off of the couch. His legs were weak and his eyes were red as blood. He slowly made his way over to the door. He unlocked the door and opened it. At this point he wasn't sure if he should let Dave in or run out of the house and jump in his car and leave. He stood there for a few seconds just looking at Dave. It was almost as if he was quietly screaming for help. Dave noticed the fear on his face but contributed it to frustration and anger from the previous night.

"What were you doin' man, jackin' off? Damn you look like shit."

Melvin walked back over and sat on the couch. He sat upright and continued looking around the room.

"I'll make you some coffee man. You look like you could really use some."

Dave headed for the kitchen.

"It was back again last night," Melvin mumbled.

Dave walked back over to the couch. "What was back?"

Melvin pulled his knees back up to his chest and started looking around again. "Something, something I can feel, but can't see. Some kind of entity I guess you'd call it. And I'm telling you man, it almost made me blow a load, too."

Dave sat on the arm of the couch and chuckled.

"Again? Let me get this right. First an alien blew you off, then Marie MacNasty and now a ghost. Maybe I do need to move in, 'cause bro you get more head than anybody I know. So this one was invisible? You mean as in ghost? Now that's a trip. As in, the ghost that blew? C'mon man, you're just still upset about last night."

Melvin sat staring at the wall, rocking back and forth. "No man, somethin' was definitely here last night."

Dave got up and placed his hand on Melvin's shoulder and spoke gently to him. He knew that he was going to need to provide him with some words of encouragement. He needed some powerful words that would help boost Melvin's confidence.

"Melvin, a ghost is not your problem. Your problem is that you're just a scared ass, livin' in this big house with the horror ho next door, man, c'mon. You know, if you lived back durin' the Roman Empire days, your name would probably be Scared-bitchius! you'd wind up bein' the 'Piss Boy' walkin' around with a huge bucket, for all who called on you to empty their hot piss in. I mean, it would have been a livin' but talk about havin' a pissy job, man!"

Melvin looked up at Dave and started grinning.

"Maybe you're right. I was a little upset after Wendy left last night and had quite a bit to drink, but man, that shit seemed so real. Scared-bitchius huh? I'd rather have the name Scared-bitchius in Rome instead of what your name would be. Cock-lickius."

Melvin pulled his weak tired body from off the couch. He stumbled into the bathroom and relieved himself. He took the bottle of aspirin from the medicine cabinet and emptied two of the round pills into his hand. He popped them into his mouth and placed his mouth under the water faucet and ran cold water into his mouth. He looked at his tired face and splashed water on it trying to revive himself, dried off then went into the kitchen for a cup of coffee.

Later that day, the guys scanned through the cable stations. The men were now bored. They had already played cards and a loud game of dominos.

"Yo man, how about a game of pool?"

Melvin asked Dave who was sitting on the couch with his foot propped up on the coffee table. He had nothing to do. He would make calls throughout the day checking on business but most of Dave's business was handled at night. He hardly ever slept. He would go to bed at two or three in the morning and still rise at about six every morning. He pulled his foot off of the table in front of him. "Sure, why not?"

The men headed downstairs to the game room Melvin had set up for his buddies. On the way to the game room they passed a room that was filled with exercise equipment. Dave stopped to look in and then began laughing.

"I'm sure this room doesn't see much action."

Melvin stopped at the room and pushed Dave in the back. "Man I work this ass out all the time. You're just not around when I do."

"Yeah, whatever Mel. Your definition of workin' out would be flippin' over pancakes, or squeezin' out ketchup onto a hotdog. Yeah, I could see your fat ass in the Olympics now, winnin' the gold in ham slicin'."

After Dave was done with all his insults, Melvin stepped into the room.

"Man, let me show you some skills."

He walked over to the treadmill that was facing the wall. It was wide with knobs and buttons, and had two large handles on each side that could be pushed and pulled. Melvin climbed onto the machine. Dave stood there with his arms folded in front of his chest. Melvin started up the machine and started walking. After about a minute, he turned the knob on the machine clockwise to increase the speed. He was now up to "mode 4" on the machine. This was the intermediate mode. He switched it back to "mode 3", then "mode 2" and continued to walk. For a guy who looked like the Pillsbury dough boy come to life, he was light on his feet and had endurance.

"I walk it out, I walk it out, I walk it out," Melvin sang as he now switched the knob to "mode 1".

"See boy, you don't know nothin' 'bout this here. You see, this is what you call, skill! And this is after bein' up all night and half hung over."

Dave stood laughing at Melvin acting the fool that he is. He was just happy to have pulled him out of the slump that he was in earlier.

"Step aside fat boy and let me show you how it's really done."

Dave climbed onto the machine and switched it on.

"Mode 4 is for pussies. There's a reason that this thing goes up to mode 7. Take notes punk."

Dave kicked it over to "mode 2". Not to be out done by Melvin, he soon was up to "mode 4". Dave was starting to sweat like a runaway slave. He still was holding his own though.

"Man I'm starting to get high from all the reefer fumes steaming from your pores dude." Melvin yelled.

Dave finally reached for the knob to pop into "mode 5". At that very moment, the room got extremely cold. Melvin could see Dave's breath in the air. All of a sudden, the treadmill knob switched up to "mode 7". This was done without any assistance from Dave, of course.

Dave's hand was pulled from the support bars. Dave's feet went back and his head scraped the console as he was forced downward. The machine threw him off. He shot off quicker than a fifteen-year-old boy with his first copy of Penthouse. His feet shot behind him, then about three feet off the ground. His face then hit the running surface of the treadmill and then the machine threw him off by his face and chest. It all happened so fast.

The next thing Melvin saw was Dave draped over the weight bench with carpet burns on the side of his face. The room was still cold. Melvin could hear the machine slowing down. He looked over at the treadmill knob and what he saw scared him something fierce. He watched the knob on the machine switch from "mode 5" all the way down to the off position.

Being the true friend that he was, Melvin slowly turned and then ran out the door and up the stairs as fast as he could.

He grabbed his keys and ran out of the house to his awaiting car and jumped in. He started the car. He couldn't move. He knew that he couldn't leave Dave like that. He was hurt and unconscious. No, he couldn't leave him like that. Melvin reached into his pocket and pulled out his cell phone. He pressed the three numbers quickly.

"911," the voice answered.

"This is Melvin in the car, Dave is in the basement. He's fucked up. I'm not."

That's all Melvin could get out before he put the car in drive and sped off. Melvin drove to the Red Lobster restaurant down the street from his house. While driving, he continued to give the operator all the information she needed.

"I'm not goin' back without backup. I told his ass there was somethin' in that house. He didn't believe me. I bet when his ass wakes up, he'll believe me now."

Melvin rambled on. Minutes after the call, he saw a police car speed by followed closely behind by an ambulance.

Melvin followed the ambulance back to the house. After arriving, he was met on the front porch by one of the police officers.

"Are you the person that called? Are you the homeowner sir?"

Melvin walked up the stairs.

"Yeah, I called and I own the place too, but not for long. I'm gettin' the hell out of here. Somethin's in there, man. I tried to tell him. I tried to tell his ass. It's not my fault! Hell, had me believin' that I was crazy. Who's crazy now?"

The police officer walked up to Melvin. He spoke to him in a calm yet stern voice. "Sir, I need you to calm down. I need you to tell me what happened? Is someone still in the house?"

"Somethin' busted his ass! That's what happened. He didn't believe that it was real so it showed him. Plus he was showin' off and shit and I think that pissed it off even more. Tore his ass up!"

"So are you saying that somebody is in the house? Are they armed? Is it a man or woman, sir? Is your friend being held hostage?"

"Man, look! Aint nobody in there armed and I don't know what it is. I don't think it's a man or woman; I just don't know. And it aint holdin' him or nothin' 'cause he is knocked the hell out!"

Just then two more police patrol cars drove up the driveway and out jumped three more officers. The officer speaking with Melvin reached down to his side and unsnapped the strap which secured his weapon. Melvin looked down at the handgun.

"What you gone do with that? That aint gone do shit. You can't shoot what you can't see. Sheeeeit, you better call Ghost Busters or some damn body! Get that little midget poltergeist bitch in here. This house needs to be cleaned!"

The officer stepped into the house. Melvin and the two paramedics stayed outside.

"He's gone get his ass busted, too. Hey officer, why don't you wait for your boys? They're comin' up the stairs now."

The officer continued on. Shortly after, he returned to the door waving the paramedics in.

"You two better get on down there. The place is secure."

"That's what you think. This place aint secure man!"

The officer signaled Melvin to follow him inside. The other officers stepped inside and went upstairs. Melvin was as nervous as a butt naked virgin looking up at a ten incher. Cautiously, Melvin stepped inside. He kept looking around nervously.

"Sir, I need you to tell me exactly what happened?"

Melvin explained how he was on the treadmill, then Dave and how the knobs moved on their own. He went on about how the room got cold and Dave getting thrown off and how he ran.

"So you're saying it was an accident sir?"

Melvin just stared at the officer. "I don't know what you would call it, but I..."

Before Melvin could finish one of the paramedics ran up the steps and entered the living room.

"Is he gonna be alright?" Melvin asked.

"He'll be just fine." the paramedic replied.

"He's got a couple of broken bones and a concussion, but he'll be okay. We're going to have to take him with us to the hospital though."

Melvin nodded his head and continued talking with the officer. It was reported as an accident. Melvin couldn't convince the officer that a ghost had tried to hurt Dave.

He followed the ambulance to the hospital and waited until he was able to go back to see Dave. Dave was a little groggy still, but could talk.

"You believe me now?" Melvin whispered in his ear.

Dave slowly turned his eyes over to Melvin. His mouth was wide open and was like a desert and his breath smelled like a combination of burning tire rubber and used kitty litter. Dave slowly shook his head. He turned his head further and whispered to Melvin. "It was just a fluke accident man, nothing more."

Melvin frowned up and turned his head. He attempted to fan the warm mustiness from his face. As I said, he was a true friend.

After wiping his hand under his nostrils, Melvin continued to try to comfort Dave. He continued talking to him to help take his mind off of the pain and discomfort.

"Man, you know, I haven't seen you move that fast since grade school. Remember? Yeah, you remember how you used to sprint back and forth through the schoolyard trying to impress the girls. Your ass would be worn out by the end of the day. Every time you liked a girl you'd do that same stupid shit. Run past her as fast as you could to show her how quick you were. Oh yeah, you were a fast little bastard, but how much pussy did you get? NONE! All you ever got was leg cramps and a pulled hamstring. You were probably too tired to fuck after all that damn runnin' anyway. Hell, I thought you had asthma for an entire year because every afternoon your ass was out of breath. Yeah, you were stupid.

I remember when Janet Parker tried several times to give you her phone number, but your ass just kept blazin' by her too fast. You'd run by and she'd yell out '581'. You'd blow by again and she'd yell out more numbers '170'. By the end of the day, every motha fucka in school had written down her number thanks to your dumb ass. Everybody had her number but you."

Dave rolled his head over in Melvin's direction and forced out a few words. "You know I hit that. Tenth grade," then fell asleep.

He inhaled then exhaled deeply. Melvin caught a slight gush of the cat ass and hot mustard mix that haunted him from the opening in Dave's face. He realized that it was time to go. Using his hand to fan the air, he cautiously retreated as not to wake Dave, and then returned to the waiting room.

CHAPTER 15   ONE FOR THE TEAM

Melvin stayed at the hospital until they moved Dave into his room. He watched over him for a while then went home.

"Perhaps Dave's right. Maybe it was just a fluke. I just don't know. There's been too many strange goin's on in that house."

Melvin pulled up to the house and hesitated before entering. He was still afraid. After trying to convince himself in the car, he still had his own doubts. He stood on the front porch for several minutes then placed his key in the door.

"I could suck the meat right off that bone! C'mon big boy you know you want it."

Marie was back at the fence yelling as usual.

Melvin thought to himself, "Um, I could have her go in first and if anything eats her ass up it'll surely die."

Melvin stepped back from the door and waved to the shadow near the fence. "Hey Marie, whatcha doin' over there in the dark woman?"

Marie stepped closer to the fence into the light. She looked hideous. She had dyed her hair orange. It was in an unsuccessful attempt to color it red.

"I'm playing with myself. You wanna do it for me?"

Melvin winced at the idea of her and him doing anything. He stepped onto the top step and leaned over the banister.

"Uh yeah, yeah I could do that for you. Come on over."

"It's about time that you came around. I knew you wanted it. You wouldn't be related to your uncle Cleveland if you didn't. Don't worry about going where your uncle's been, hell, dogs do it all the time."

Marie turned and walked along the fence toward the gate. She talked to herself and yelled out more obscenities the entire time. She walked around the front of the house and then up the driveway. When she reached the steps that led to the house she strangely looked around. She placed her foot on the bottom step and paused once more then she climbed up the remaining steps.

Melvin stood at the top of the steps. He unzipped his jacket and pulled it opened and down his arms in an attempt to take it off. Right then, while his arms were incapacitated, Marie grabbed his crotch and started rubbing his unit. Melvin started to feel sick. "Hold on Baby, let's wait until we get inside, your old man might see us."

"My old man?"

Marie kept her hand on Melvin's crotch. She took a drag from her cigarette and then plucked it into the yard. "I guess I can work with this," she said as she stepped into the house.

Marie walked inside and stripped down to her birthday suit and headed for the kitchen. "Whatcha got to drink around here?"

Melvin stood there praying not to hurl. The bile was doing the "Cha Cha Slide" on his stomach. She was even more nasty looking than he had imagined. Melvin could hear her pouring some type of liquid into a glass. He turned and noticed that his television was on. He didn't remember it being on when he left, especially not on the "Lifetime" channel, but with all the confusion who knows. He leaned over and picked up the remote and turned the television off.

"Hey bring me a double of whatever you're drinkin'," he yelled. "And try not to drip on anything while you're in there. As a matter of fact, make that a triple."

Marie stepped out of the kitchen holding the two glasses. Her skin looked like Roseanne Barr had borrowed it and had returned it all stretched out. Her breasts lay nice and relaxed flatly against her chest. Her butt was as flat as an ironing board, she had about twelve long gray hairs on her chin and her ribs protruded out like a fossil in the sand. Her toe nails looked as if they had never been cut. She had a huge wart on her knee with hair growing from the top and her vaginal area was bumpy and contained small dents covering it as if it was beaten with a bag of nickels.

"Hurry up baby, let's get this party started!"

Marie switched on the radio and started dancing around the room. Melvin sat down on the couch and downed his drink. He started thinking of ways now to put her out. "What about your husband?"

Marie kept on dancing and singing. "He's not my husband. You don't have to worry about him I hope. He's just something that the wind blew in. Come on, get those clothes off!"

Marie danced over to Melvin. She placed her arms around his neck. Melvin took the glass from her hand and downed her drink, too. She climbed on top of him and started grinding. She puckered up her lips and leaned towards his face.

"Kick in liquor, kick in damn-it!" he was screaming in his mind. "How about one more drink baby?"

Melvin pushed Marie back and rushed into the kitchen. He grabbed the bottle of rum and turned it up to his mouth. He filled the glasses, took another gulp from the bottle then slowly returned back to the couch.

Marie was still on the couch on her knees playing with her breast. Melvin sat back down and passed Marie her glass.

"Look here Baby, I can't do this. I have to get up early in the mornin'. How 'bout a rain check?"

Melvin was now slurring, the alcohol was starting to take effect. She placed her glass on the coffee table and leaned back on Melvin.

"Well that only means one of two things big boy. You're either getting up early dehydrated and worn out, or you're gonna over-sleep from being too dehydrated and worn out. Take your pick!"

With that, Marie jammed her tongue deep inside Melvin's mouth. She continued to kiss him hard. He tried to pry her off, but she held on to the back of his head. She was locked on like a leech. He could taste the liquor and cigarette mixed saliva pour into his mouth.

As she moved her tongue in his mouth, he started to feel her dentures. They were loose and moving up and down against his teeth. Melvin tried not to vomit in her mouth, but he could feel it coming. He closed his eyes.

He was trying his hardest to pretend that she was Wendy. He placed an image of Wendy's face on top of Marie's. That was the only way that he would be able to see this through.

While Marie held on to the back of his head with one hand and unzipping his pants with the other, Melvin weakened. It seems that the liquor had finally taken completely over.

He was feeling good and drunk now. Marie saw that Melvin had no fight left in him. She let go of his head and used both hands to unbuckle his pants. She reached down into his pants and grabbed his member. She slid down to her knees and yanked on his pants until she got them down to his ankles. Then after pulling off his shoes, she slipped his pants off.

She leaned forward and took his member into her mouth. It was unbelievable.

Melvin was moaning out of control. He reached down to run his hands through her orange hair and noticed her dentures lying on the coffee table. She had pulled them out soon after dropping to her knees.

At that second, visions of "Polygrip" denture glue matted to his pubic hair floated through his mind. Those thoughts popped in, then were dismissed very quickly by Marie's superior oral skills.

"Damn, toothless head, now that's a concept. I might have to stick old girl. I mean, who'll know. If the head is this vicious, the ass has to be outrageous! No wonder Uncle Cleve was hittin' this shit. This head is off the hook!"

Melvin started rubbing her back. Then, without warning, the room got cold. Marie paused for a second and then started going at it harder and faster. Melvin could see his breath again.

"Ding! Ding Dong! The doorbell startled both Marie and Melvin.

"It's your mean friend; he's going to shoot me. He said that he would if I came over here."

Marie jumped up and grabbed her clothes. The warmth returned.

Melvin jumped up and slipped his pants back on.

"Melvin! Melvin, are you in there?"

It was Wendy. Melvin looked puzzled and walked over to the door. He looked over at Marie, who was now fully dressed and looking pissed. Melvin opened the door.

"Wendy, what are you doing here?"

Marie walked up to the door and stood beside Melvin. Wendy looked at Marie and then over to Melvin.

"Did I catch you at a bad time?"

Melvin looked at Marie then opened the storm door so that Wendy could enter. He grabbed Marie by the arm.

"Fucking whore wasn't gonna let me finish anyway," she said.

"Uh yeah, we'll have to finish that game of scrabble another day Marie. Wendy, meet Marie. Marie, Wendy. Marie was just leavin'. Bye Marie, talk to you tomorrow."

Marie snatched her arm from Melvin. She sashayed her narrow body over to the coffee table and picked up her teeth and walked back up to him.

"I won't be back. It's got a thing for you. It wants you. Just like your uncle and it's jealous, too. I'm not about to go up against that!"

"Well right on and ten-four good buddy, over and out!"

Melvin grabbed Marie's arm and led her to and out the front door.

"What was that all about?" Wendy asked.

"She a bit touched, so I try to help her out by letting her stop by. You know, play cards and shit like that with her. Enough about her, what are you doing here?"

Wendy sat down on the couch and took Melvin by the hand.

"I felt so bad about the other night that I just wanted to make it up to you. My cell phone got shut off, so I thought I'd stop by and see you in person."

Melvin realized that this was the most opportune time to see exactly where Wendy was coming from.

"How much do you need to turn your phone back on? I want you to always be able to contact me."

Wendy slipped her shoes off then leaned forward and slid her jacket off. "You're so nice Melvin, but I couldn't ask you to do that. Oh, I hope that you've forgiven me for the other night. Sorry I freaked out on you."

Melvin looked away thinking, "Damn, maybe I was wrong about her."

Melvin gently slid his hand down the side of her face. "Forget about the other night. Look, it would be no problem, but I understand. You want to be an independent woman."

Wendy pushed out a fake smile and looked away. "I mean, you know, if you really want to turn it on, it's cool. I mean, I do need it and all."

"How much is it to turn it on?"

Still looking away, Wendy pulled one of her hands from Melvin's and started scratching her head. "I mean, I haven't paid the bill for a minute and I use text messaging quite a bit. I think it's something like seven twenty."

"Seven hundred and twenty dollars? That's not text messagin', that's what you call writin' letters!"

Wendy continued scratching. She wouldn't make eye contact with Melvin.

"I mean, you could give me the money and I could go get it turned on tomorrow morning. It would really help me out."

Melvin saw her then for what she really was, a gold digging stank ho who was trying to hustle him.

"How you gone hustle a hustler?" he thought, but then decided to play her game. Get what he had always been after and then leave her alone. Watch her plan backfire.

"Cool, I could do that. What you gone do for me though?"

Melvin leaned toward her. He started kissing her and went right for her breast. He no longer had the need to pretend that Wendy was in the room. He had the real thing.

Now kissing her savagely, Melvin started to wonder if she had placed someone else's face on him to get her through, because now she was kissing him back.

He unbuttoned her blouse and pushed her bra up forcing her breast to pop out from the bottom. He paused for a second to get a good look at what he had wanted to see for such a long time. They really weren't what he expected but would do for the night.

She leaned forward and placed her hands around his neck. He held both her breasts firmly in his hands. Melvin could now feel his heart pounding through his erection. He felt her gently stroke his member and then slide her hand deep between his legs. Melvin reached down and unsnapped his pants then slid down his zipper. He needed to do nothing else. Immediately he felt the warmth from her hand squeezing and tugging on his hot flesh. The slow but constant stroking was making him quiver. Melvin pulled his head back just far enough to whisper. "Hold on baby, don't make me blow a gasket just yet."

The room started getting extremely cold again. Wendy removed her hands from around Melvin's neck and started rubbing them together to warm them. Melvin placed both of his arms along the back of the couch and continued enjoying the gentle massage.

With his eyes still closed, he could hear Wendy rubbing her hands together. The rubbing then stopped abruptly. Melvin cracked open an eye and peeked over at Wendy. She was looking down at his crotch with both her hands covering her mouth. He then noticed that the massaging had not stopped.

Melvin slowly looked down and could not believe what he was seeing. The skin on the shaft of his penis was moving up and down. It was as if he was masturbating with no hands. Wendy revved back on the couch. "How are you doing that? Boy, you are so nasty."

"Well you pulled it out."

"No I didn't. I'm not touching that thing."

She rose from the couch. She reached over and retrieved her jacket from the coffee table. Once again, Melvin sat there looking extremely embarrassed. He tucked himself back into his underwear and pulled up his pants. He stood there for a second collecting himself. Then he realized that both of Wendy's hands had been in fact, around his neck the entire time.

"Melvin, I've got to go. Furthermore, I did not come here for that. I really like you Melvin, but you've got some serious issues. Now, how about my cell phone bill? You're still going to take care of it aren't you?"

Melvin, standing there looking puzzled asked, "How about that ass? You can't get something for nothing sweetheart."

Wendy buttoned up her jacket and put on her "upset" look.

"Oh, it's like that, huh? I thought you cared about me Melvin. So you just want to pay me for sex, is that what it is?"

Melvin dropped his head and started looking at the floor. Wendy continued laying into him. She knew that he felt bad about what had happened.

"I'm no prostitute Melvin. How dare you offer to do something for me and expect sex in return? Is that what you want? You want to pay me to sleep with you like I'm nothing more than a common ho?"

Melvin continued looking at the floor like some little boy who had just been caught by his mother for peeking in her room at her tits. He managed to muster up enough nerve to mumble out a few words. "If you're sellin' it, then uh, yeah I'm buyin'."

He knew this would piss her off, but what the hell, he knew she didn't really want him for anything else but money anyway. Wendy walked up to him. He braced himself for the slap that he knew was coming. She raised her hand and slid it under his chin and raised his head.

"How much?"

Melvin looked at Wendy with a confused look.

"How much are you willing to pay? I'm sure we could come to some agreement. You do have all of that money now. You'll need somebody to spend it on won't you? For the right price, you can get it whenever you want."

Melvin's whole world came crumbling down. The woman of his dreams was just a common ho. He couldn't believe it. He looked at her totally different from that second on.

"I don't know," he said with now, a very cocky attitude. "Why don't you drop down on those knees and suck on this so I can see what its worth. You do give head don't you? I've got to make sure that you've got what I need before agreeing to this deal. Hell, the pussy, too. I've got to see if it's poppin'."

Wendy backed off and started pointing her finger at Melvin. She then started moving her head wildly as she spoke to Melvin.

"Let me tell you something Mr. Melvin. All the money in the world couldn't put a down payment on this pussy, but it is for rent and if you can work it right, maybe we'll consider it as a lay-away plan. I've gotta go right now, but you think about it and when you want to do some serious business, you call me. Put some money in my hand and I'll give you a sample. You got five hundred on you right now?"

"Nope, but I'll call you when I do."

Melvin walked over to the door and opened it. Wendy left.

CHAPTER 16   CONTACT

Melvin sat back down on the couch; thinking about what had just happened and everything prior to that. He thought about the statements that Marie had made during her departure. He knew that she must have dealt with whatever it was in the house with him before. Maybe while she was with Uncle Cleve she had experienced it, too.

"It didn't hurt Unk and it hasn't hurt me yet either," he thought.

He looked around the room. Convinced that there was a presence in the house, Melvin decided that it was worth a chance to try and communicate with the entity. He got up and positioned himself close to the front door for easy access, in case he needed to make a quick get away. He collected himself. Nervous, he began to speak, calmly and quietly.

"Uh, look here. I know you can hear me. First of all, know this, I come in peace. I don't want any trouble nor am I here to bring harm to you. I know what you're capable of, after all, I saw what you did to my boy Dave. That was messed up though. And I know it's been you doin' those things to me, too. I'm not quite sure why, but I aint complain', you know. Now you know black folk don't usually do the stay in the haunted house type thing, but I can live with this just as long as you don't hurt me or anybody else. I mean, hey, can't we all just get along? It was you who took me those nights, wasn't it? I guess that's what you like to do. And to be honest, well, I like it, too."

Nothing happened. Melvin inched his way deeper into the room. He, for some reason, no longer felt as afraid. He tipped slowly back to the couch then lowered himself onto the cushion.

"You got a name?"

Melvin sat there feeling somewhat like an idiot. He looked around the room and asked his question once again. "I say you got a name?"

There was no response. Melvin continued looking around the room. "You just gotta stop with the sneakin' around. Let's just be straight up. You're a ghost. I get it. I live here, too now and I'm not goin' anywhere. I take it that the pink room and all that old shit is yours? That's cool and I can respect that. You gotta realize though that I aint leavin'. Hell, I got nowhere to go. So what I'm sayin' is that I can deal with you if you can deal with me. How 'bout it?"

Still Melvin got no response. He sat on the couch with his hands tucked tightly under his thighs. Suddenly, the room got cold and the walls started getting damp. Melvin's pants were yanked opened and his zipper snatched down. His pants and underwear were pulled down to his ankles and without notice he was taken.

He was pulled and sucked and scratched for over an hour, and since he could not see her, he couldn't tell if she was sucking him or riding him or what. He enjoyed every minute of it. When it was over, Melvin lay tossed across the couch. He was spent. He reached over and pulled a half of a joint from the ashtray that he had been saving, and lit it.

"I take that as a yes? That's what I'm talkin' 'bout. I can handle that. Like I said, I'm not sure why you like to do that, but I'm glad you do. This can turn into a great friendship if you let it. Just give me a chance. You can trust me. I'm not about to blow this. It's the perfect arrangement and that head is all that! I like that thing you do with my balls, too. I've never had that done. To be honest, you're the best that I've EVER had. You want a hit?"

Melvin lit his hand rolled cigarette and then took a few puffs from it. He held it towards the ceiling.

"You sure you don't want to hit this? It's some good shit. Hey, you never told me what to call you."

Of course he knew that he wouldn't get any response. He rested the smoking rolled cigarette in the ashtray that sat on the coffee table in front of him. He bent over and pulled his underwear and pants up to the edge of the couch.

He arched his pelvis then pulled them up to his waist then snapped his pants shut. As he zipped himself up, he watched the twisted refer cigarette drift into thin air then stop just in front of the big chair next to the couch.

The tip of the refer cigarette's flame flared as he watched the arc in a downward motion. After sitting for a second, it reversed direction and streamed up and out towards Melvin. This action was repeated before the cigarette was returned to the ashtray.

"Oh, so I see you understand the puff, puff, give standard operatin' get high protocol huh? So can you speak? Maybe you don't speak my language. I'll tell you what, since you won't tell me your name or can't tell me, how 'bout I give you one. Let's see."

Melvin sat there thinking as best he could. The marijuana had him floating. He sat giggling as he thought of crazy and stupid names. He thought of names that he knew would get him killed. Names like "Ghost Bitch" and "Invisible Good Head Giver" until it hit him.

"I've got it! Ok, check this out. I know how you love that room and since you love that room so much and you have a thing for pink, how about Rose? Rose! Yeah, I think that would suit you just fine, a soft, sexy, fiery rose."

For the next three days the sexual attacks continued to occur randomly and Melvin welcomed them. He made it a point to never wear underwear because he wanted to make sure that Rose had easy access to his precious jewels. He even attempted to cut a hole in the center of his sweatpants for "reach in" access but

Rose continued to pull them down. Plus his testicles stayed cold all the time from the draft.

This morning was no different from the rest. Melvin had just been awakened by his early morning "dawn buster". She would come in, take care of business and then vanish without warning. She always made sure that he was satisfied before her departure.

Melvin climbed out of bed. He could hear his phone ringing downstairs. He put on his slippers and rushed down to answer it. Coughing and clearing his throat, he answered.

"Hello."

There was a long pause then the voice calmly spoke.

"Yo man, what's up? Why haven't you been by? I've been askin' about you. I know you just didn't leave me hangin' like this. What's up? How are you doin'? You're not trippin' off of this are you? Look here, I'm goin' home today, stop by and holla at me. And bring me somethin' to eat, maybe a steak and cheese. I've been eatin' this nasty hospital food and I need somethin' to re-establish my newly sanitized taste buds. Hook me up man."

It was Dave. Melvin hadn't been to the hospital to see him since that night. He was so busy enjoying his new amusement.

"Man, I've been pretty busy. You know, busy takin' care of things around here and all. Why don't you come on out here to recoup?"

"Too busy? That's not you. You've been to busy to come holla at me? Huh uh, somethin"s up, what's goin' on with you man?"

"Nothin' bro. I just got hung up on some things and thought I'd get things squared away by the time you got out. Plus you know my head was in a bad way after that night. I had to deal with that man, 'cause I wasn't right."

"You ok now? Have you gotten yourself together? I don't need you freakin' out on me man."

"I'm straight, did some thinkin' and some lookin' around in here. It took a couple of days, but I'm together now. So, you recoupin' out here or what? I'll hire a young sexy chick to come wait on you hand and foot 'til you recover."

"Nah, gotta see what's goin' on with my goods, you know. I expect to see you today though. Take a break and stop through. That damn house aint goin' nowhere."

"I'll be there."

Melvin hung up. He took care of a few things around the house then jumped into the shower. He got dressed, grabbed his jacket and keys and headed for the door.

As he reached for the knob, he could feel the cool wind flow from upstairs. He pulled the door opened and looked back. Quickly, the door slammed shut.

"Aw hell nah! Not now! I gotta roll. I'll be back. You can hit it then. I'm just runnin' over to Dave's for a few. He just got out of the hospital that by the way, was your doin'. I haven't seen him since he went in. I'll see you when I get back. Well, maybe not see you, but feel you. Keep it warm 'til I get back Baby. See ya!"

Melvin grabbed the door handle. He could feel a strong force pulling him back by the back of his pants. The room got bitterly cold. Melvin could feel his pants being pulled down from behind. He was being tugged so hard that his feet were off the floor behind him. His pants were now down to his hips. He could feel the bitter cold making its way down the crack of his butt. He was then thrown so hard onto the couch that it slid about six feet across the floor. His hands were pinned back and he was taken orally until he was drained of his fluids.

After this ordeal, Melvin got up and adjusted his clothing. He picked up his jacket and started for the door. The room was still freezing. He turned the knob and pulled. He pulled again as hard as he could, but could not open the door.

"Alright Rose, enough! You had your fun, now let me out."

He then tried the back door. The results were the same. He walked back into the living room and picked his cell phone up off the floor. He dialed Dave's number. After four rings he answered. "Yeah, what's up?"

Melvin looked around the room then down at the floor as he spoke into the phone. "Uh, I, I can't make it man. Uh, somethin's come up. I'll try to make it tomorrow. If not, then I'll call you tomorrow."

"You alright man?"

"Uh, yeah, yeah, I'm alright. I just got somethin' I gotta do."

Dave knew that this wasn't like Melvin at all. He knew something was wrong.

The warmth then returned to the room. Melvin went upstairs and laid across his bed in the fetal position. He felt like a two-dollar ho. Tired, sore and dehydrated, he drifted off to sleep.

Three days had passed and no one had heard from Melvin. His days now consisted of laying on the couch in a pair of pajama pants with no underwear for easy access. He had become a personal whore. The attacks had increased in frequency and Melvin never fought back. He was too weak.

Melvin was doing his usual today. Sitting on the couch half dehydrated and watching the Jerry Springer show. There was a loud knock on the door. Melvin's eyes lit up. No one had been by for days. He hadn't made any calls and every time his cell phone rang, he got molested orally. He finally just shut it off. He climbed off the couch and tried the knob. It turned.

He opened the front door and found a young blonde FEDEX delivery guy holding a brown box. This was the same guy who had delivered packages on several occasions. He knew Melvin's face and Melvin would often offer him a beer or other beverage. Melvin could see him standing there displaying his "I'd like a beer" smile. With the storm door still closed, Melvin motioned him to leave the box on the porch. The man's smile faded and a look of puzzlement replaced the once cheery look. The man pulled out a small digital contraption and slid it along the side of the box. He then picked up the clipboard that was lying on top of the box.

"You'll have to sign for it sir," he yelled through the glass.

Melvin slipped his feet into his bedroom slippers and stepped onto the porch.

Melvin signed the form while he inched closer to him whispering. "Help me. Can you give me a ride? I need a ride. Shhhhhh."

The man looked at Melvin strangely. Melvin leaned his head over to the side and looked inside the house with his eyebrows raised.

"Look man, how many times have you delivered here? Never mind that, I'll give you fifty bucks to get me outside the gate, no make that a hundred. You know me, and you know I'm good for it."

The guy continued to look at Melvin puzzled.

Melvin continued, "Man, just get in the truck and start it up and we'll discuss the rest later. Look man, this is a matter of mistaken identity, life and death, hell, national security even. Now go start the damn truck."

The young man nodded and started back down the steps. Melvin picked up the box and waved.

"Have a nice day man, hey, and thanks a lot."

The man climbed up into the large step van. He turned the key and started the truck without hesitation. The large sliding door was wide open. Melvin began perspiring harder than Jessie Jackson at a Klan rally. He dropped the box and sprinted towards the van. He dove in yelling, "Go! Go!"

The van pulled off. They raced down the driveway and onto the street. Melvin had lost one of his slippers during his escape, but that was the least of his worries. Melvin sat on the floor of the truck and leaned back against the wall looking out through the large opening in the back. He looked at the driver through the metal cage that separated them.

"Thanks man. That bitch is crazy. Thank you so much."

"Woman problems, huh?"

"You don't know the half of it."

"I hear you. What happened, another woman?"

"I wish that's all it was. Nah, just one woman. She just wants me to stay home and be her sexual slave all damn day. She won't let me breathe. Every time she gets upset with me she sucks me dry. Every time I want to go somewhere she slams my dick in her mouth. My phone rings, blowjob! And on top of that, she's a deaf mute."

"Wait, let me make sure I understand you. Your woman doesn't speak and loves blowing you off, especially when she's mad at you, and you're upset with that? Dude, you need a roommate?"

Melvin didn't answer. They continued to dodge through traffic. Every time the driver tried to slow down, Melvin would encourage him to go faster. The van had just turned onto King Street in Old Town Alexandria. Melvin could feel the chill starting to fill up the cargo area of the van.

"Stop! I think you'd better let me out right here."

The van came to a screeching halt.

"You sure? I can take you wherever you need to go."

Melvin jumped out the back of the truck looking around before speaking. "Nah, aint no need in both of us gettin' fucked up. Thanks man, you may have just saved a brotha's life. I'll catch you on the next delivery for your dough. I'm good for it right?"

The driver held up his hand and popped up his thumb.

"No problem dude. You gonna be alright?"

Melvin stood looking up and down the street clenching the chest area of his sweatshirt.

"Man, I'm standin' here with pajamas bottoms, no underwear, a sweatshirt, one shoe, a wedgy so deep in my ass that I'm coughin' cotton, no money, somebody's after me that I can't even see, and it's colder than penguin piss out here. Uh, that would be a BIG FAT NO! And buddy you don't even want to know what's goin' on in my life right now. Let's just say that right now, it sucks to be me!"

Melvin was feeling that chill still.

"You'd better go man. You'd be safer away from me."

Melvin walked past the passenger side of the van. The driver leaned over and handed Melvin a five-dollar bill, wished him good luck and headed down King Street.

"I'm not goin' back, if that's why you're here," Melvin was saying to himself. At least that's how it appeared to all who passed by him. Melvin just kept talking. He didn't care who was looking. He could feel himself being pushed or tugged on as he walked.

Then Melvin yelled out, "I will not be a prisoner in my own house!"

People on the street were now watching his every move. Melvin quieted down and limped off. He approached a group of people who had formed a line at the bus stop. Melvin got in the back of the line. He tapped the woman in front of him.

"Excuse me ma'am, does this bus go into D.C.?"

The woman turned and looked him up and down. She nodded her head and turned back around. After standing there shivering for about ten minutes, he could see the bus approaching.

The bus pulled up and the people began to pile on. Melvin was approaching the door when he heard someone yelling.

"Hold the bus!"

Melvin asked the driver to wait and a young girl, no older than sixteen ran up to the bus. Melvin waved her in front of him and she started up the steps only after looking at him strangely. He felt the chill grow stronger.

As she made her way up the steps she was stopped in her tracks. She had one hand on the metal bar railing and the other on the metal pole at the top of the last step. She looked down at her hand that seemed to be stuck. Melvin knew that she wasn't stuck. He felt the cold chill.

"No Rose. Leave her alone. This is between you and me." He whispered.

He went to help her, but only made it to the bottom step. He too now could not move either. She looked back at Melvin as she felt her skirt being hoisted over her buttocks. She tried to pull it down but could not.

Melvin could see the string of the thong underwear that she was wearing. He was locked in on the flesh of her backside. He tried to look away, but being the crack hound that he was, he could not tear himself away. He could see the flesh on her backside being squeezed and rubbed. This went on for a minute before her skirt lowered. He knew what was happening.

He knew it was Rose. She was trying to set him up. She was trying to make him realize that she could make his life a living hell. The young lady looked at Melvin. He was standing there with a stupid looking smile on his face.

"You pervert! I'm calling the police," she yelled and quickly rushed back to a seat with her face red as a hot tamale. Melvin still could not move.

"Let me go! Let me go Rose!"

Now yelling, Melvin was once again looking as if he had just escaped from a mental institution for the criminally insane. Suddenly a man approached the bus. He was a strong looking athletic type carrying a gym bag. Melvin stood there hoping that somehow the young man could help him move from that spot. He was still stuck.

As the young man neared, he looked down at Melvin. He nodded his head in greeting.

Melvin then asked, "You gettin' on man?"

Melvin still glued to the pavement, motioned him in front of him. Before he could speak, there was a loud "whoosh!" Then the cold surrounded him. The man smiled, thanked Melvin and proceeded up the steps of the bus. The cold rushed up the stairs once again, this time behind the young man.

"Oh shit!" Melvin mumbled. "Don't do this. Ok Rose, you win. I'm goin' back!"

It was too late. The man was now motionless. Melvin watched him try to snatch his hand loose from the rail, just like the young girl. His bicep bulged with every pull. He then saw the man's pants gather in the back then draw up at the legs. It was as if someone had a hand up his crotch. Then his pants moved up and down in the back and he could see the man's butt being squeezed.

"Ah damn, now this is gone be an ass whippin' that I just don't need. Take it like a man Mel, just take it like a man."

The man was released. He turned and looked at Mel. Melvin closed his eyes in anticipation of the impact. He opened his eyes and the man leaned forward and extended his arm. In his hand he was holding a small rectangular card. Melvin reached out and accepted the card from the chiseled young man. He leaned in and whispered to Melvin.

"This is my card. My cell number's written on the back. Call me anytime."

Melvin stood there still. He looked in through the doorway and saw the bus driver on his radio reporting the incident. Melvin tried to apologize as the doors closed in his face. He was then set free and the movement in his legs returned. Quickly, he turned and limped back in the direction from which he came.

Melvin stopped and looked into the window of an antique furniture store. He could see the window mist up as he peered in. Now cold and hungry, Melvin was trying to keep his tears contained. He had run out of options.

"Okay bitch, okay, you win you bitch!"

Melvin stood on the curb looking pitiful. He watched the oncoming cars race by and even considered stepping in front of one of them.

The gunshots rang out so loud that they made Melvin jump. At least that's what they sounded like. "POW! POW!" the loud short bursts kept popping louder and louder until they sounded as if they were right up on him. He could feel the squeaking sound from the brakes piercing his ears before it stopped.

"Señor Malveen! Is dat choo Señor Malveen?"

Melvin slowly looked up into the window of the smoking contraption. It was Mr. Carlos, sitting in his loud shaking pickup truck with his oversized straw hat on.

"Where are you going Señor Malveen? Choo need a leeft?"

Melvin said nothing. He just nodded his head and limped over. The door to the small pickup truck opened and there sat Mr. Carlos along with his wife and four of his kids all piled in the front seat. Melvin slowly turned and limped towards the back of the truck. He climbed in the back bed along with the lawn equipment and the dog that smelled of lawn mower oil and wet chicken. He found an old sack filled with top soil and leaned against it.

While sitting on the cold truck bed floor he could feel his freezing sack shrivel up seeking the warmth of his body. The dog walked over then lay next to his bare foot. He sniffed it for a second before he started in on it. He licked the bottom of his foot then made his way up. He started licking between Melvin's toes as if it were a meal...

"Guess you got a thing for salt huh?"

The canine continued. Mr. Carlos poked his head out of the window to make sure he was situated. His kids looked through the rear window at Melvin as they giggled. His wife smacked them on their legs and forced them to turn around and leave Melvin alone.

"Choo okay amigo? Choo don't look so good."

Melvin remained speechless. He slid his wet slimy naked foot away from the dog and folded his arms across his chest. The dog remained in a lying position and inched his way back over to his tasty treat and resumed licking. Melvin was too tired to move anymore. He just hoped that the dog wasn't hungry enough to start biting his salt covered flesh. He leaned his head back and closed his eyes.

"Dats okay Señor Malveen, I get you home. I get you home right away."

Mr. Carlos put the truck in gear and after several backfires from the engine, off they went.

Upon his arrival, Melvin slowly climbed out of the pickup bed. The dog stood and escorted him over to the side of the truck. After kicking his legs over and placing his feet firmly on the ground, the dog licked the side of his face. Melvin looked at the canine and smiled.

"Thanks man. As if I was already having a bad enough day as it is, now I have dog tongue, salty feet and flee infested dog ball musk on the side of my face."

Carlos stuck his head out of the window.

"Choo going to be okay?"

Melvin nodded and thanked him. He waved to Carlos and his wife and kids as they backed down the driveway. Melvin thought that was strange of him but then realized that Marie was sitting in her yard. Mr. Carlos didn't want to take the chance of her yelling anything to him in front of his family.

After Mr. Carlos had clicked and backfired his way down the driveway, Melvin realized that the only person that could possibly help him make any sense out of all of this would be Marie. She knew something. She knew when Rose was there on the night that she was pleasing him. He remembered the comments that she had made as she left that night.

He walked over to the fence that separated their yards. Marie was sitting on a concrete bench next to the matching birdbath that sat in her yard. She seemed to be scribbling something down on a small yellow notepad and humming to herself.

Melvin placed both his hands on two of the cool metal bars and then whispered, "Marie? Marie, can I speak to you for a minute? I need to talk to you Marie, real bad. I need your help."

Marie looked over at Melvin then back to her pad. "You should have thought about that earlier. Back when you were treating me like trash. Oh I was good enough to satisfy your freaky urges but just don't let nobody know huh? Just like all the others. All of you men are just alike. I knew you'd be over here. Asking me to help you, just like him."

"Him who, do you mean my Uncle?"

"Him, too. He was about the only one that I could help. The others, well it was too late for them. Just like you, it's probably too late for you, too."

"What can I do? How can I stop it?"

"There's a way, and it's still in the house. You have to find it, but right now you'd better get on back inside because it's here for you. You should have fucked me."

Just after Marie had spoken those words, she grabbed her throat. It was as if she was being choked. She tried to speak but could not. Suddenly, she was forced to the ground. She laid there whimpering. Melvin then felt surrounded by the cold. He looked at Marie once more then headed for the house. He climbed the steps then hesitantly approached the front door. His legs felt weak and shaky. He knew that he was going to be punished for his attempt at freedom and possibly for talking with Marie. He slowly reached for the knob of the front door. Without his assistance, the door opened.

Melvin looked back down the steps wondering if he should try to flee again, but knew that it was useless. He turned back, took a deep breath and stepped inside. The house was dark and a stiff chill surrounded him.

"Ok, I told you, you win. I'm tired, just tired."

The door slammed shut.

Melvin walked over to the couch and kicked off his remaining shoe. He sat there with his head resting on one of the fluffy decorative pillows that was lying on the coffee table. The warmth returned and Melvin welcomed it. Rose did not punish him. She was just happy to have him back in the house. Melvin sat thinking, trying to make sense out of what Marie had said to him.

"It's still in the house. What's still in the house? I rearranged every room in this house, every room except..."

He continued thinking until he drifted off to sleep.

CHAPTER 17   THE BATTLE

The next morning Melvin woke up, but not in his bed. He woke up naked in the back room. He found himself surrounded by the pink walls that he hated so much.

The furniture that he had disposed of filled the room. Everything was back in its original place. Melvin slowly rose to his feet. "Look, you can't hold me prisoner here. That wasn't the deal. And what, were you expectin' me to stay in here? No way!"

Melvin started looking around the room. He opened drawers and looked through the closet. He didn't know what he was looking for, but whatever it was, he knew that it would be in that room. He dug through the drawers. He only found old clothing and rings and such.

"I know you don't expect me to dress up in this bullshit! I am not a slave. No, I refuse to put this crap on. If you're gone kill me, go ahead but I aint puttin' those clothes on."

Melvin felt a strong jolt and then he was smacked and slammed into the wall. His bare bottom was continually slapped as if he were getting a spanking. Melvin backed himself against the wall.

"Damn you're a violent old ho!"

He then heard the clothes hangers in the closet begin to rattle and clang. The old eighteenth century clothing began to fall from the hangers onto the floor. Hats and other garments from the top of the closet shot out as if they were launched from cannons.

That's when he saw it.

On the top shelf of the closet he noticed a small box. The box had a small lock on the outside, on top of the lid. Melvin made his way over to the closet. He quickly slipped on the old colonial clothing.

"Can a brotha get some socks? My feet are kinda cold."

He reached up and pulled the box down from its resting place. The room filled with the cold damp air and Melvin was knocked to the floor. He did not try to get up. He just drew his knees up to his chest and placed his arms around his legs crying.

"Ho, you obviously don't know who you're fuckin' with. I am Melvin D."

Before Melvin could complete his sentence he was pushed across the floor and into the wall on the opposite side of the room.

"Oh it's like that huh?" he yelled.

He got up and walked back over to the box.

"Alright, I'll put it back."

He picked up the box and raised it above his head and started in the direction of the closet. Just before reaching the door opening, he threw the box forcefully to the floor. The box shattered.

There, on the floor was what appeared to be a small straight whistle. It was a dog whistle made from wood; at least that's what it looked like. There was also a small envelope with beautiful calligraphy scribed on the front. Melvin looked at it strangely then quickly fell to his knees and picked up the whistle. He was then thrown back up against the wall. He slid down the wall to the floor holding his head.

"Damn, what a day I'm havin'." Melvin knew that there was something to that whistle. Maybe it was what Marie had told him was in the house. He lay on the floor debating if he should take the chance and blow it.

Melvin rolled over to his knees. He inhaled deeply then slipped the whistle in his mouth. Before he could push his breath into the small device, he was thrown against the closet door. He continued holding firmly to the whistle. He knew that it was something that Rose feared. It had to be what Marie spoke of, Uncle Cleve's weapon.

Melvin lifted the whistle and quickly blew into it. What he heard after that frightened him more than being thrown around. It was the highest pitched squeal that he had ever heard. The room returned to a bearable temperature. Melvin rose to his feet. He walked over and picked up the envelope, pushed out his chest and strutted out of the room. He started yelling at the top of his lungs.

"So you don't like that, huh? I told you that you didn't know who you were fuckin' wit' BITCH! What's that Chuck Brown used to say? Get yourself a whistle and blow!"

Melvin started singing the words to an old "Go-Go" song by "Chuck Brown" and blew that damned whistle until he was safely in his car. As he placed his key into the ignition, he could see Marie standing by the fence holding her ears. As she lowered her hands from her ears, Melvin blew the whistle once more. She pressed her hands over her ears again and looked around to see where the sound was coming from. Only there was no sound. "Well I'll be damned! I guess it does work on ghosts and dogs!" Melvin chuckled.

He pulled the whistle out of his mouth and drove off while continuing to sing the Go-Go song.

"Get yourself a whistle and blow, dunt-da-dunt, any kind of whistle just blow, da-da-dun-dunt. Ooh, ah, ooh, ah."

He pulled up around the driveway and stopped. Marie stood at the fence with her hands still near her ears, but not covering them. Melvin yelled to her.

"I found it! Thank you baby, I owe you one."

Marie smiled. She removed her hands from her ears and then placed one between her legs before yelling back to Melvin.

"And you'll pay, too. Pay dearly you will. You're gonna fuck me. Yep, that'll be payment enough. Fuck me good, too you will."

Melvin frowned up his face and pulled off still singing the words to the song. "Get yourself a whistle and blow…"

Melvin was gone for hours. He did not have any visits from the entity the entire time that he was out. Melvin returned home with groceries and beer. He stepped in the house happy and loud.

"Honey I'm home!" he yelled.

He went into the kitchen and put away the groceries and shoved the beer in the fridge. He went back into the living room and sat on the couch.

"Okay, bring your ass out here. We need to talk. It's time to renegotiate our contract damn it, since you couldn't adhere to the terms of the old one!"

Nothing happened. Melvin pulled out the whistle that now hung around his neck, attached to a brand new necklace.

"Okay, if you want to play hardball, I guess I'm gonna have to just blow my little friend. Now, I've read the letter. You know the one from Lord Ressein or however you pronounce his name. It seems that you were sought out back in your day. Sought out and captured in this very house for committing a crime. You had committed a crime involvin' the violation of a young man's virtue. I couldn't really make out some of it, but I did get that part. So I figure, what? You were probably a school mom or somethin' of that nature. I believe you, with your overwhelmin' desire to suck the venom out of any Virginia black snake young or old, probably drained the life out of some poor young innocent fool and his parents found out. How far off base am I? I also read about the head injury that you got durin' the beat down and how after which, you were able to hear the high-pitched sound of dog whistles. The same whistles that were blown over and over to keep those dogs on your ass, a whistle like this. It's hard to believe that they beat and killed you, a woman and for what, givin' a blowjob? That sucks. Sorry, no pun intended. I didn't mean to go there. I mean, suckin' is what got your ass stretched out. I gotta tell you though, my ass bleeds for you. You do know that shit happened a long time ago? And yet you're tryin' to take that shit out on me. Don't blame me, I wasn't even thought of at the time. Hell, my great grand-daddy wasn't even the makin' of a hot nut yet."

The air in the room chilled then turned into a wind. It blew briskly and grew in intensity. It whirled around and throughout the living room, getting stronger and stronger until it finally died down. Melvin knew that Rose had heard every word that he had spoken. He somehow also knew that Rose was now thinking back. Thinking back on the events that now had her captured in this house and unable to let go of those terrible memories. He too began to visualize what must have taken place there. He now, could no longer move. He could feel her near him. He could feel her touching him, but different than usual.

He could now hear the sound of the dogs barking and the wooden wheels of the coach approaching. He could hear the gallop of the horses racing up into the yard with angry men wearing triangular shaped hats and ruffled blouses. Angry men, angry men who wanted only to do her harm and who wanted her blood.

He now understood that Rose was making him see. Making him see what actually happened on that awful day. Melvin stood there, still and quiet. He was hardly even breathing. He could now see the steam from the nostrils of each horse as they were yanked and stopped abruptly. How the men grabbed ropes and whips to torture the woman who had shamed their children.

After forcing the door open only to find her hiding in her room surrounded by the pink walls and a large doll collection. Melvin watched them drag her into the front yard to beat her. Blowing those piercing whistles for the dogs to attack, bringing her to near death. He watched them kick and beat her until she was unconscious.

Melvin thought it was now over. Then he couldn't believe what he was seeing. He couldn't believe how callous and heartless these people were. He watched the men lift Rose up from the blood soaked ground. They draped a rope over the thickest limb of the big oak that still stands tall in the front of the house. One end was tied to the saddle of one of the horses and the other around her neck. She was hung. After her limp, lifeless body was no longer swaying from her jerking, they all unloaded their weapons into her flesh.

Melvin slowly returned from his trance. He now felt a new compassion for Rose. His gently brushed the tears from the corners of his eyes as he felt her presence leave.

"Get back in here! It was wrong for them to do that to you. Those men were as crooked as a dog's hind leg. I'm sure they all burned in hell for their wrong doin's. You've suffered deeply, but that doesn't give you the right to fuck me over."

Melvin soon turned back into his old self.

"I mean a blow job here and there will work, but those ass whippins', hell nah. This is a new day Baby, and I haven't done a damn thing to you. You've been on this damn power trip for too long. THAT SHIT'S OVER ROSE!

I'm the man of this house. This was your place, but for whatever reason you moved the hell out. Ok, you got kicked out, but death is just as good of a reason as anything else. You still didn't pack your shit though, but we'll discuss that later. I don't mean to sound like such a heartless bastard, but like I said, I am the man of this house. This shit is mine. So bein' that I am the man, the owner AND I've got this here little whistle, I'm the boss! So get your ass in here before I get to blowin!."

Melvin placed the whistle to his lips. The temperature started to drop.

"That's my girl. Now listen up! If you want to get along, we can get along. If you want to fight, well then let's get it on. You have been a real bitch. You're jealous, selfish, and inconsiderate. This was fun at first until you had to turn it into some kind of power trip. Now that I've got this little whistle, that kind of evens things up. Oh, and by the way, the chain is welded and it's too small to fit over my head, so don't try it. So do you want to work this out or what? I come and go as I please damn it. You got it?"

Melvin sat and waited. Nothing happened for a minute or two. He then felt himself being gently and slowly pushed back against the couch. His pants were opened as he was fondled and caressed. Melvin realized that Rose understood that they were now a couple. She no longer had control over him. It was as though she appreciated his dominate attitude. This time, Rose didn't take Melvin. She slowly satisfied him. After having his fluids completely drained, Melvin sat up.

"Right on baby, that's what I'm talkin' 'bout. Let's do this!"

Several weeks had gone by and Melvin was having the time of his life. Dave was feeling better and finally able to leave the house. Melvin had called him periodically to check on him and had gone by to see him several times, but this was the first day in a while that they would be able to hang out. Dave wanted Mel to meet him at The Sapphire that night. Melvin got dressed and was singing as he started down the steps.

He grabbed his jacket and yelled, "I'll be late, don't wait up."

The room chilled. Mel turned and pulled on the doorknob. The door would not open. He stuck the whistle to his mouth and blew, turned the knob and walked out.

"See you in a few," he yelled as he headed to the car.

Melvin couldn't wait to see some of his old friends. Melvin drove singing to the music from the radio and tapping on the steering wheel. He pulled into the parking lot of The Sapphire and jumped out of his car still singing. He opened the door and the music poured out into the air. Melvin walked in dancing to the music. He saw Dave sitting at the bar in his usual spot with some of the old crew.

Melvin sat down beside Dave, grabbed his hand and embraced his friend.

"What's crackin'?" Mel yelled over the music.

Dave leaned over to one side on the stool and grunted.

"My ass. That's the only thing that's crackin'. Man I've had the worst gas since I've been out of the hospital. I don't know what's up with that. How you been man, haven't seen you for a minute, everything alright?"

"Yeah, things are ok now. Had a rough couple of weeks but everything is fine now. Hell things were so rough for a minute, this is the first day that I've actually had a bath in three days."

"Wait, let me get this right. For the last three days, you've been smellin' like hair, armpits, ass, AND feet? Damn, I'm glad you didn't stop by. You seen your girl?"

"Who?"

"There she is, heard she's been coming in here quite a bit, too."

Melvin looked over to where Dave was pointing. There, standing by the D.J., was none other than Miss Wendy. She saw Melvin, too. She waved and started making her way through the crowd.

"Hey stranger! You never did call me."

She placed her arms around his shoulders and gave him a tight hug.

"Yeah, I know. I've been pretty busy. You know how it is."

Wendy slid her hands down Melvin's arms and took him by the hands.

"So you're seeing somebody, huh? Wrote me off with the rest, huh? Nobody's heard from you at the job either. Don't tell me that you've gotten too good for us common folk."

Melvin let go of her hand, turned and waved to the bartender.

"Uh, yeah. Yeah, I met somebody."

Wendy let his other hand go and touched his face. She gave him a kiss on the cheek and whispered in his ear. "I know you're not fucking that little old shriveled up thing that lives next door to you, and what about our deal?"

"What deal? I told you that I'd call you when I had the money. I changed my mind. Look woman, I been chasin' you for years then all of a sudden, I come into some money and you're ready and willin'? Man, what a let down. All this time, I've been chasin' a hoin' ass trick who basically sells pussy. That's just so disappointin'."

"No Melvin, what's disappointing is finding you in your house with a nasty little woman who looks like you picked her up off the street. Having her in your home and doing whatever to her. Oh don't think I didn't hear you moaning when I walked up. That's what's disappointing, and down right nasty. You ought to be ashamed of yourself. You mean to tell me, you'd rather screw that homeless woman than to make love to me?"

"Look woman, I told you that she was my neighbor. I wasn't hittin' that. The only thing you heard was her givin' me a massage, that's it! I would have loved to have tapped that ass of yours, but you just got too much game. You had it then and you got it now. You've got nothin' to offer me woman. You're a slut Wendy, a pussy sellin', no blow job sample givin' trick!"

Wendy became extremely angry, but so did Melvin. Wendy had spoken badly about Marie and Melvin didn't like it. He knew that if it weren't for Marie, he'd still be stuck in that house. After all that he had said and done to her, she had still been willing to help him.

Wendy pointed her finger in Melvin's face and with her lips tightly pushed together, she grunted out, "Your loss mother fucker," and walked away.

Dave pulled his glass from his lips and looked at Melvin.

"I don't believe it. You got a girl? Damn. She must be fine as hell if you let that sexy piece of ass walk away. So, can I have that one? Sheeit, I don't mind sloppy seconds!"

Melvin took the beer from the bartender and paid for his drink. Dave ordered another.

So who is she man?"

Melvin starting smiling like a little schoolboy then shyly answered, "She's at the house. You'll have to come out to meet her."

"Hold it! You've known the ho for a few weeks and she's already moved in? Boy, don't tell me you're pussy whipped already. See, I can't leave you outta my sight for one minute! How's the head?"

Melvin looked over at Dave but said nothing. He just started smiling. Dave started smiling, too. Dave took another sip from his drink and looked back over at Melvin again.

"Word? It's like that?"

Melvin nodded then both men busted into laughter and started giving high fives. The men talked and drank for hours.

"Look man, I gotta go, why don't you stop by tomorrow?"

Dave downed his drink then burped.

"You damn skippy I'll be there tomorrow. I've got to see the ho that turned your ass out! Damn man, she got a sister or a girlfriend? Hook me up."

Dave started laughing. They pounded fists and Melvin left.

CHAPTER 18   IN SIGHT

Melvin had arrived back home. It was just after 3 a.m. He pulled in front of the house and staggered up the stairs. He and Dave had really tied one on. He pulled out his keys and fumbled with them for a few minutes trying to get the key into the small opening. He turned the key and pushed the door. It would not move.

He turned the knob back and forth and pushed against it with his shoulder. He realized that it was Rose. She was pissed. He pulled out his whistle and tried to blow, but could not. He could only manage to fill it with his saliva. He tucked the wet device back against his chest and pressed his face against the door.

"Open up Baby! Rose! Open the door!" He yelled over and over.

This continued for over twenty minutes and still Melvin remained locked outside of his own home. Melvin, now holding his crotch and twitching as he paced around the porch was furious. Not only was he locked out, he was cold, and his bladder was about to explode. Melvin pulled out his cell phone and dialed Dave's number. The phone seemed to ring forever. Finally Dave picked up. With his voice weak and hoarse, he answered.

"Whoever this is, this shit better be important."

Melvin rushed over to the end of the porch, pulled out his penis and started to relieve himself.

"Yo Dave, I'm on my way over," he slurred. "Rose locked me out man. Seems she thinks that I was out with some woman or somethin'. Man, I don't know what's wrong with her some- times outside of bein'… Oops, I almost gave it away. Actually, this is the first time that I have ever really cared about what a woman thought. I guess she doesn't realize just how much she really means to me. But anyway, I need you to stay awake long enough to open the door, 'cause I'm locked out man. I mean standin' here pissin' over the porch rail type locked out. So can you do that? You can stay awake for me, can't you? You're my boy and you always got my back, of course you can do that! Huh Buddy?"

There was a long pause on the phone.

"Dave? Dave!"

There was still no response. Then Melvin could hear the low roar of the chain saw sound, that of snoring. Dave was asleep.

"Damn!" he shouted and staggered down the stairs.

He walked over to the little stone boy statue and fell to the ground beside him. He now began discussions with him. "Man, what's up with women? I mean you just can't do right by them, even when you love 'em. You ever have problems wit your lady? I doubt it. Havin' a stiff hard stone erection all day, everyday, probably keeps her mind off most things, huh?"

He pulled himself up by the bowl then looked up at the little boy.

"Ah, what the hell."

Melvin leaned forward gripped onto the little boy's buttocks, and took a sip from his flowing stream.

"Don't you tell anybody bout this. This is just between you and me buddy but I must admit this piss of yours is pretty darn tasty. It's refreshin', too! What kind of diet you on? It's like spring piss. I mean, don't get me wrong, I'm not a piss drinker, but most piss smells horrible. Not yours though, it's hittin' the spot."

While drinking, Melvin felt the familiar chill brush by him. He looked up at the house. The front door slowly opened.

"It's about time woman, got me out here drinking pee. Good pee but piss just the same."

Melvin looked over at the little stone figure and continued slurring. "No offense man, but piss is piss no matter how good it is."

Melvin stood upright, and headed for the house. He climbed up the stairs and slowly stepped in. With the chill now surrounding him, Melvin placed his hands on his hips and looked around the room. "Bitch! What in the hell is your problem? Why'd you leave me out there so long? You've got some splainin' to do."

During his slurring of profanities, he could feel his crotch being rubbed. He slowly looked down, and mumbled...

"But I can forgive you."

Melvin sat down on the couch and struggled to take off his jacket. Once off, he slung it across the coffee table. He leaned back and Rose started in. He could feel his belt being tugged on. He leaned forward and grabbed on to his pants.

"No Rose, not like this. Not tonight. I want to make tonight special. I want to make you feel good tonight."

Melvin got up, kicked off his shoes and started up the steps.

He walked to bedroom at the end of the hall. Now accustomed to the pink walls and furnishings, he walked in. He lit a few of the candles and lay on the bed. The chill followed.

"That's right, that's right, I want you tonight Rose. Not just a hand job, or some of that smokin' head, which by the way, should be placed in the Oral Hall of Fame, but not tonight. Tonight I want to feel you. I want to be inside you. I want to at least feel what I can't see for once."

The air grew colder. Melvin stood up and disrobed. He slid back on the bed. "How about I just point it at the ceilin', and you can just crawl all over it," he whispered. Melvin could feel his legs being pulled toward the edge of the bed. He pushed himself back up to a sitting position, but continued to lean back. He then felt her presence. He felt the weight of her body on his legs, as if she were straddling him. His penis was then positioned at an angle and gripped tightly. Melvin braced himself. He then felt the head of his penis begin to penetrate her small opening. It was tight. He didn't push at all.

After gently working him inside, Rose began thrusting hard. Melvin gripped the edge of the mattress as he moaned uncontrollably. "Oh damn baby! That's right. Ride me, oh that's it, ride me! Ride me like a damn pony."

Melvin was being humped and ground. The stroking was now increasing in speed. Rose was now pumping him faster, and harder. Melvin was doing everything possible not to blow his load but he felt it coming. He wanted Rose to get all she wanted, but he couldn't hold on. Just then, he thought of Marie.
Not only did his load retreat, but he was losing his erection, too.

He quickly shoved Marie's ugly ass out of his mind, and focused back on Rose, who was now moving like a wildcat. Suddenly, with one hard thrust, Rose shot off of Melvin like a cannon. A strong cold wind blew out every candle in the room. The room was now dark, but warm. Rose had left him sitting there.

"Hey, you just gonna leave a brotha hangin' like this? Rose, where you at girl?"

Melvin remained sitting on the bed for another twenty minutes or so still hard as a rock. He got up, gathered his clothing and went into his room. He chucked his clothes in his laundry basket and turned on the shower. He stood looking at himself in the mirror smiling.

"Yeah, I tore that ass up, didn't I girl?" he said, nodding his head and speaking proudly.

Melvin stepped into the shower. He couldn't believe what had just happened. He had actually boned a ghost. He jumped out of the shower still thinking about his miraculous feat and scrubbed himself all over.

Then he thought, "Damn, did they have STD's back then? Hell, I think George Washington died from syphilis didn't he? Damn, I knew I should've worn a condom."

Melvin stepped out of the shower and dried himself off. Still feeling the effects of the alcohol and marijuana, he dismissed his negative thinking and went back to him being the man. He eased his way back to his bedroom. He climbed in his bed and began to smile still thinking about Rose.

"Who's turned out now, bitch?!"

He turned on his television set and dozed off still smiling.

As always, the next morning, Melvin was awakened in the normal fashion. Rose was sucking the life out of him. He was squirming and moaning loud enough for Dave to hear as he approached the front door. Dave stood on the porch listening, waiting for Melvin to bust his load before he knocked. Melvin finally yelled out. "Oh you fuckin' bitch! Now that's how you deep throat a motha fucka!"

Dave stood at the front door giggling for another minute while he finished his cigarette then tapped on the door. He yelled up at Melvin's window.

"Melly Mel, open up man. It's me, Dave."

Dave stepped back and looked over at the fence. To his surprise, there was no Marie. For once she was not at the fence or hanging out of her window yelling out to him.

"Well I'll be damned. I don't believe it. Her syphilis must have finally eaten through her ass and killed her."

Dave advance back to the door and began to knock once more.

Melvin sat up on the side of the bed. He looked around the room. "Okay, what's the rule? We don't hurt Dave, right? I trust you on this Rosie. He's my boy. He's my best friend. He's about the only one that I can trust with this, so you listen to me. Be nice, ok?"

Melvin slipped on some sweats and a tee shirt and headed downstairs. He opened the door to Dave's big smile, and both of his thumbs thrown up.

"You the man! I could hear her servin' you up from down here. Deep throat, damn I'm jealous. I've never been deep throated. Damn, you sure I can't borrow her for just one night?"

"Man, get your ass in here and shut the hell up."

Dave stepped in and immediately started looking around for Rose. "Hey man, you know this is the first time that I've come over here and that old crazy, nasty lookin', walkin' piece of shit wasn't at the fence yellin' her head off. Rose didn't have to beat her ass did she?"

"Who you talkin' 'bout, Marie? Ah man, she's not so bad once you really get to know her."

"You didn't? Tell me you didn't. Tell me you DID NOT stick YOUR pecka in that little nasty escapee from Oz! You did, didn't you?"

Melvin frowned up his face and shook his head trying to hide his guilt, but he knew that Dave could always see right through him. Dave stared at him shaking his head.

For a minute he did not speak. Finally, he managed to push out the only words that came to mind. "Nasty Motha Fucka."

Melvin waved his hand in the air at Dave then turned his head. "Man you're crazy, aint no way. She's just nice, that's all, a little crazy, but nice."

"Yeah, nice enough to give your dick gangrene, but hey it's your dick."

Dave walked over and sat down on the couch. He placed his hands on his knees and started tapping a rhythm out on them.

"Okay, where is she? Wait, don't tell me that Marie is really named Marie Rose and you now call her Rose. Is that why I didn't see her grindin' the bars on the fence, because she was upstairs grindin' your ass? Yuk!"

Melvin started laughing while pointing over to the fence then back at Dave. "That's real funny man, hilarious even. No man, Rose is Rose and Marie is…"

"Is a nasty stank ho that I believe you banged, you nasty bastard!"

"Dave! Dave! Can you just get off of Marie for a second? Damn!"

"Can you? If I find out that you… Damn, you'll never hear the end of it Mel, NEVER!"

Dave leaned back on the couch. He folded his arms across his chest, still frowning.

"Look Dave, there's somethin' about Rose that I need to tell you before I let you meet her. It might be a little hard for you to understand. I need for you to trust me and listen."

Dave placed his hands back on his knees.

"Well you don't have to tell me about how good that head is. I mean, the entire neighborhood knows now, after listenin' to you screamin' like an old bitch this mornin'. Hell, I gummed up my underwear just listenin' to y'all. If y'all ever want to swing or need a third party, I'm your man! As for trustin' you, up until you lied about bangin' the skinned cat next door, that went without sayin'. So what's up?"

Melvin stood reminiscing and smiling to himself. He walked over and sat next to Dave.

"Dave, remember when I told you that there was something here, in this house? Remember?"

Dave looked at Melvin uninterested and then picked up the remote control.

"Yeah, I remember. You were trippin'. Thought a ghost had slung me off of the treadmill and was givin' you head every night. Now I know you're not going to tell me that you've got a Gremlin upstairs that's making you scream. If that's the case, I'm going to throw it in some water right now. Doesn't that make them multiply? Hell, I only need two or three of 'em."

"No, I wasn't trippin'. You see, it was that same somethin' that messed up my date with Wendy. It was that same somethin' that, well let's just say, caused your accident. And it is the same thing that has been makin' me the happiest man that I've ever been in a long time. It's Rose."

Dave looked at Melvin puzzled. "Just what in the hell are you sayin', man? Stop bullshittin' and just lay it out. This is me. You got somethin' to say…, say it. You know how it goes with us."

"I'm sayin', Rose…, Rose is, uh, I guess you would put it, not of this world. Rose is a ghost. There. Now. I've said it."

Dave did what he always did. He laughed crazily.

"So let me get this right, you're sayin' that the person who just finished makin' you sing soprano upstairs a minute ago is a spirit? She just appears and gives you a blowjob and then disappears? So I guess she'd be what you'd call a Head Fairy, huh? So what do I need to put under my pillow to sing like that? Yeah, right Mel. So what's this Rose look like? Does she have like huge big tits, and a nice ass, or is like a ghost ass… invisible?"

Dave started laughing again. Melvin, realizing that he had never seen Rose, not even a picture of her, was speechless. He felt like a real idiot.

"I really don't know. Like I said, she's a ghost you fuckin' moron."

Dave stood, and laughed harder. "Let me get this straight. You're tellin' me that a ghost has turned you out and you've never seen her. So you're like, the Ghost Buster! Yeah right. How come you've never seen her? Look man, tell that ugly bitch from next door to bring her ass on down here. Don't worry, I won't tell anybody, anybody that you don't know that is. No really, your secret is safe with me. So your girl Wendy was tellin' the truth, huh? She did catch you two, huh?"

"It wasn't like that and stop callin' Marie those names. I told you she was cool. She helped me out, that's all."

"Helped you out? What, you needed to release some of the backed up semen in your body? If you have a ghost girlfriend then, what does she look like? You haven't told me yet."

Melvin looked at Dave then slowly around the room.

"I don't know. I've only imagined, but I truly don't know."

Dave went back over and sat beside Melvin. He placed his hand on his shoulder.

"Seriously Mel, are you okay? Are you really serious about this? If so, let's make a deal. You bring the ghost ho out right now and you two can live happily ever after with my blessin' and support. If you can't bring her out, which means that she's just a figment of your imagination, then you let me take your crazy ass to Washington Hospital Center right now to get you some help. Deal? I mean, listen to you. What would you think if it was me tellin' you that I was havin' a love affair with a ghost?"

Still staring off into space, Melvin mumbled back, "Yeah, I guess you're right. I guess I do sound a bit crazy, huh? I thought I was too, but then she… Uh, yeah, yeah okay, deal. She'll do that for me. She'll come out."

Melvin wondered for a minute if he really wanted to know what Rose actually looked like. Dave kept nudging him on his arm.

"What's up man? What are you doin'? You tryin' to figure out what size straight jacket you wear? You look like about a 3x to me, maybe a 4. Are you callin' her out with that … what you call that shit? Telepafy?"

Melvin pulled himself out of his deep thought. He looked over at Dave shaking his head disgustedly. "It's telepathy dumb ass, and I'm not crazy, you'll see."

Melvin started looking around the room. Dave watched Melvin closely then did the same. He too, started scanning the entire room. Only he had no idea what the hell he was looking for.

"What are you lookin' for? I don't…"

"Shhhhhh, as a matter of fact, just shut the hell up until I'm through."

Melvin continued looking around then began to call out to Rose.

"Rose? Rose Baby? I need you. I want you to come out and meet Dave. He doesn't think that you are real Baby. C'mon Baby, I need you. If you don't show yourself, I'm afraid that I'm gonna have to believe him, too. Hell, maybe I am crazy. Maybe I just want you to be real. C'mon Baby. Come on out, please?"

Melvin was beginning to look sad and confused, and for once, Dave didn't crack a smile. He was really concerned for Mel. He knew right then that Melvin wasn't kidding. He really believed that there was a Rose and that he really needed help. Dave placed his arm on Melvin's shoulder. "Don't worry man; we'll get you some help. I'll be right by your side. Maybe you just wanted Wendy so much, you made Rose up. That's understandable. A lot of folks with money go crazy. We'll get you some help buddy."

Melvin turned to Dave. His face looked pitiful. It was as if someone had just waked him from a bad dream.

"How do you explain the attacks, and me bein' locked out, and you bein' thrown from the treadmill?"

Dave stood up. He shoved his hands deep into the front pockets of his hooded sweatshirt.

"Well Melvin, nobody really saw these attacks but you and as far as you bein' locked out, well you were drunk remember? You were probably tryin' to open the door with the wrong key man. The treadmill was just a fluke accident."

Melvin placed his head in his hands.

"Maybe you're right Dave, maybe I do need help. I guess I should make an appointment for tomorrow. Damn, she seemed so real."

Just then, the room got cool. Melvin lifted his head and started smiling.

"Oh hell nah, I'm not crazy. See? You see? She's here."

Dave popped his hood up and covered his head. He returned to the couch and sat by Melvin and started looking around the room. He looked at the vents and then smiled.

"No man, again, explainable. Your furnace is either shutting off, or you air conditioning unit is turning on. I'm sure if we walk downstairs, we can find a reasonable explanation for this. Is this what you're basing your ghost theory on? C'mon man."

Melvin kept smiling and looking around the room.

"No man, you're wrong. C'mon baby show him. Please? If you don't I'll have no choice but to believe that he's right - that I'm crazy. Rose! Do this for me. Show yourself to me. I don't care what you look like, Baby you will still be my lady."

Dave, now looking at Melvin like he just fell off the short yellow bus, pulled his hood down. He was feeling sorry for Melvin. Suddenly, a glowing light appeared in the corner of the living room. Both men stared silently at it. The light shone from the floor, then very slowly up the wall. As the light made its way upward it left behind a clear image, first, one foot then the other. Dave slid closer to Melvin and placed his hand on his gun.

"What the fu… Is that her?" Dave asked with a trembling voice.

"Yes, yeah that's my Rose."

Dave turned his face to Melvin's. They were so close that their faces were almost touching. The wind blew throughout the room. That's when Dave took his gun out. Melvin looked at him sitting there holding his nine millimeter and began to laugh.

"Don't worry, she won't hurt you."

Dave placed his gun down on the table.

"Well in that case, I don't mean no harm man, but the bitch got some big ass feet, Bro."

Melvin didn't care about that. He just kept his eyes focused on her image. The light traveled even higher. The images of legs then waist, stomach, and chest were revealed. Dave turned to Melvin again. "Mel, again, I aint hatin' or nothin' man but, your ho got some big ugly hairy legs. Plus she aint got no tits either man. And uh, I might be trippin', I mean I do have glaucoma and all, but are those crushed up balls that I see bulgin' out under that dress?"

Melvin continued looking and smiling.

"She's got tits man, they're just dense."

"What? Are you saying that her tits are too stupid to appear?"

"No dumb ass, I mean dense as in… ah never mind. See, I'm not crazy."

"Sheiiiit, who says? I think you are crazy for sleeping with that!"

The light was gone. The entire image of Rose was before them. Rose stood there in a pair of leather clog shoes, thick stockings, and a dress from the late 1700's. It was ruffled and had lace around the neck and the bottom of the sleeves. Her hair was wavy and lay against her shoulders.

"She's ugly," Dave whispered to Melvin.

Melvin was no longer smiling. Dave turned and whispered to Melvin again.

"She's got huge hands, too."

Rose stood there smiling. Melvin stood up and walked over to Rose. Rose was taller than Melvin, too. Dave walked over and stood behind Melvin. He yanked on Melvin's arm trying to get his attention. Melvin slowly backed up several steps and leaned his head over to hear what he had to say.

"Uh, look here cuz, I don't mean no harm, really I don't. I mean, I think it's cool, you know, you bein' with a ghost and all, but uh… Did you notice that Rose, well Rose… aw fuck it, Rose has a damn Adam's Apple! There I said it. Looks like that Rose apparently has a thorn that she aint told nobody about, if you catch my drift. Actually, your Rose looks more like a Russell, but that's just me. But don't mind me. You know my eyes are all messed up. You know with my glaucoma, I still need laser surgery and glasses. That's the only reason why I smoke so much weed."

Melvin looked at Rose from head to toe. He moved in closer. Rose looked at Melvin strangely.

"May I touch you?"

Rose's image then became more vivid. She slowly nodded giving him her approval. Melvin swung his arm back low beside him and then forward quickly and jammed it into Rose's crotch.

"Motha fucka! I can't believe this shit. You've got a buck and two quarters just like me. Ah man. Ah hell no! You're a man! I thought you were a woman who was just ugly as hell, but you're packin'."

Melvin was so angry he could have exploded. He held his fist up and shook it at Rose.

"If your ass wasn't already dead I'd kill you. Dave, you're right! She's a man, and with a dick bigger than mine!"

"Well that's ninety nine percent of the population. Hell, I know some women with bigger dicks than yours, too. He didn't happen to pop you, did he Mel? You didn't get fucked did you? You know like bein' on the receivin' end? Any end has got you labeled but when you're fucked, you're fucked. Now that one would be hard to explain. I mean we go back to 'red light, green light' and all, but you gettin' poked by a man… Ghost or no ghost, I just don't know man. That would put a big strain on our friendship."

Melvin looked back over at Rose, Russell or whatever its name was.

"You disgust me!" He yelled out.

He placed his hand over his mouth to avoid vomiting. Then for the first time, Rose spoke.

"I tell you the same as I told your forefathers. Do you think that I chose to be this way? Do you actually believe that I wanted to be spat on and ridiculed all the days of my life? No.

Living like a hermit is not a life that anyone should have to endure. After finally finding someone who loved me for me, I was punished to save his reputation and honor. I was castrated, hung, stabbed, and burned. So therefore I ask you, who are the strange ones? Is it right to pass judgment on everyone who is different than most? I'd rather be the way that I am than to be like those hypocrites who sit in church and pray to their God then despise all those who aren't exactly their like. Damn you all!"

Then in a flash, the image vanished followed by a strong wind that blew through the house knocking down pictures and moving furniture. It was like a small tornado had passed through the room.

The wind was now blowing even harder. Rose was insulted and hurt. Dave was laying face down on the floor holding his knife. Melvin reached down and retrieved the metal whistle from his neck. He blew as hard and long as he could. Suddenly, the glass of the living room window shattered from the strong blast of wind. Seconds later, everything settled.

It was quiet. It was now calm.

"She's gonna, what in the hell am I sayin'? I mean, he's gonna fuck your ass up now boy," Dave yelled out.

"No, I've got somethin' for his ass!"

Melvin pulled out his cell phone and made a call. They got up and walked outside to the front porch.

"Let's go Mel. Let's get the hell out of here."

Melvin walked over and sat on the top step.

"Hell no, I aint goin' nowhere. He better find a new place of residence. You hear that? I can't believe that punk was suckin' on my Johnson, and I actually…"

Melvin leaped up and leaned his head over the banister and vomited.

"Look Dave, we go way back right?"

Dave nodded his head.

"So we can just keep this between us right?"

"You know that man. This shit never happened. I didn't get my ass whipped and thrown off no treadmill by no ghost and you didn't bone one either. Deal!"

Melvin and Dave sat on the front porch for almost a half hour. They could hear the engine of the truck backfiring up the driveway. It pulled in front of the house where the guys sat. Melvin walked down to the truck and hopped in.

Mr. Carlos sat there and nodded his head as Melvin spoke. Minutes later, Melvin got out and Mr. Carlos pulled off. Melvin walked back up the stairs and into the house. Dave remained on the porch. He could hear Melvin picking up the thrown debris and moving the furniture back in place. Still Dave would not enter.

"Hey Dave, can you come give me a hand?"

Dave stood up and walked toward the door.

"Man I'm not coming back in there. Man that was some scary shit. Hell no!"

Melvin walked to the front door and opened it slightly.

"Well if your monkey ass is gonna stand out there for the rest of the evening, how about I pass you a lantern and a jockey suit and you go stand on the front lawn? Let me see that little Sambo smile of yours."

Dave saw no humor in Melvin's statements. He turned and sat back on the steps. Melvin finished picking up and putting things back in order inside. It took him a couple of hours, but he managed to get things back the way they were. From the living room he could hear the truck's speedy return. He stepped outside.

After the truck had come to a stop, Melvin trotted down the steps and stuck his head through the window of the passenger side of the vehicle.

"You got it?" Melvin asked.

Mr. Carlos passed him a contraption and Melvin handed him two crisp one hundred dollar bills.

"It works very good Señor Malveen, it works real good. I hope it is to choo satisfaction."

"Thanks Carlos, I owe you big time man."

Mr. Carlos nodded and sped off. Melvin returned to the house. He went into the kitchen and grabbed his screwdriver from the red and gray plastic toolbox that he kept under the sink. He mounted the contraption on the wall with the two screws that Mr. Carlos had given him. Melvin walked upstairs and down the hall to now Russell's room. Melvin opened the closet door and lifted the paint can from the closet floor. He pried open the can and turned toward the wall. He slung the paint over every wall in the room. He continued to pour paint over the furniture and floor. He rushed back down the hall and could feel the temperature in the hallway dropping. He could also hear the wind heading his way. Melvin looked back for a second then ran down the steps, two at a time.

He rushed over to the contraption that Mr. Carlos had made for him. The room started to chill.

"Oh you want some of me? Oh I've got somethin' for your ass, you bastard!"

The wind started to rev up again. Russell was pissed. Dave, although terrified, rushed in looking for Melvin. Just as the papers started blowing over the room, Melvin plugged the contraption into the wall socket. Dave was blown back on the porch, flat on his back by what was now known as Russell. The wind was so strong, that after he hit the front porch, he slid about another four feet.

"And don't bring your ass back here either!" Mel yelled out as he rushed to the front door.

Dave, still on his back, reached into his jacket pocket and pulled out a pack of cigarettes. He pulled one from the wrinkled pack and slipped it between his lips. He reached in his other pocket and pulled out his lighter and lit his menthol stick. Melvin walked out and stood over Dave.

"What a day I'm havin'," Dave mumbled through the cigarette.

"Well his ass won't be back."

"What is that thing Mr. Carlos gave you?"

Melvin pulled down the neck of his shirt and Dave looked up at the whistle, which hung around Melvin's neck.

"He hates the sound of this, so I had Mr. Carlos build me that box to hold a whistle just like this one. It has a compressor or somethin' like that in it that blows air continuously. I just told Mr. Carlos that I need somethin' that would blow into a whistle like this one until I shut it off. You know like a fan. Hell, I'm gonna keep it on all the time."

Dave lay on the porch blowing smoke rings then snapped his fingers.

"Hey, now that you found out that you're gay, are you gonna start wearin' those shirts that you tie up at the front bottom? Or maybe start wearin' those nut crushin' jeans? How 'bout shavin' your naval or snappin' your fingers and movin' your head when you're talkin'? Anyway, I'll understand if you say that you can't come over 'cause you're havin' your feet done."

Melvin looked down at Dave and raised his foot over Dave's face.

"I'll stomp a mud hole in your face right now. I'm not gay. I didn't know that she was a guy, so that makes me exempt. You know, and I thought we weren't goin' to talk about this anymore. It's squashed! That gay ghost did kick your ass though."

Melvin started laughing. Dave climbed to his feet.

"Yep he did, even put my ass in the hospital. And you're right, you're not gay, you're just gay friendly. Hey, Mel?"

Melvin still laughing turned to Dave.

"What, fool?"

Dave walked over to the top step of the porch.

"That Rose could suck a mean pipe though, huh?"

Melvin took off after Dave. Dave ran down the steps and out into the yard laughing.

"I'm just playin' man. I'm just playin'."

They stood by the little naked stone boy laughing. Dave took his hand and smacked the stream of water that flowed from the statue.

"Don't knock it over fool, that water's good and cold. It kinda tastes like spring water, too."

Dave looked at Melvin with a half cracked smile. "Uh, uh, no! You did NOT drink the stone piss. Nah, I'm not even gonna ask."

"I was thirsty man. It was good, too. Matter of fact, I'd put that little fella's piss up against anybody's bottled water."

"You didn't, you little nasty motha. Man what's with you? You've changed boy. I mean, first you're bangin' a gay ghost, now you're suckin' piss from little concrete boys' pricks, what's next, pumps and pocket books? You've got some real explainin' to do Mel. Or is it now, Melleesha? You got somethin' that you want to tell me?"

"Yeah, I've got somethin' that I want to tell you. They won't even be able to find your body if you keep on fuckin' with me man."

Dave popped up his two fingers forming a "V".

"Peace my brother. Damn, some people are so violent. C'mon Nasmo, let's get outta here. Let's hit The Sapphire or somethin' and put this shit behind us. Let's go anywhere; just as long as it's away from this place, it's been a rough day. You might even get a chance to buy that pussy that you passed up. What's her name, Wendy?"

"That woman aint speakin' to me, I'll give her a call though. I don't know."

Melvin and Dave walked back to the car. Melvin walked up the steps to lock the front door and rushed back down to the car. He looked over to the fence for Marie but she was still not there. He climbed into the car and they pulled off.

CHAPTER 19   THE BEGINNING

Over a year had passed and there had been no signs of Russell. Melvin had gone out with Dave the night before and had gotten pretty messed up. He drank more than usual in celebration of his one-year anniversary in the house. They had managed to put everything behind them.

Dave didn't see Melvin as much anymore. They still hung out but Melvin would still stay home for days on end, but was happy with his life. This particular night they hung out and drank as much as they could put down.

Dave had only been out of the hospital again for three weeks. This made the celebration even more special. Dave had gotten shot during a hold up. He was held up by one of the crackheads that lived in his building. How stupid. During Dave's stay in the hospital his attacker disappeared and was later found dead in the Third Street tunnel but no one seemed to care, especially Dave. He was happy to be alive, happy to keep his business running, happy to be hanging out with his ace, Melvin. That night they tied one on that they would always remember.

After his head was right, Melvin pulled out his cell phone. He selected Wendy's number from his contact list and pressed the talk button.

"Hello."

"Wasup woman, it's me Melvin, how you doing?"

"I'm doing married."

"Married? Wow, well congratulations. Sorry, I didn't know. I've kinda been out of touch."

"Well, I'm still open to our little proposition. I mean, I still could use some extra money."

"Hey, let me call you back."

Melvin hung up shaking his head. He couldn't believe that she was that low. He felt low himself, because deep down inside he still wanted to hit it, at least once. He figured Wendy still owed him from teasing him so much. Dave looked over at him.

"Damn man, you ok? Who was that, that's got you lookin' so down man?"

"That was Wendy. The bitch got married. She's still talkin' bout me hittin' it though, but I don't know."

"Don't do it man trust me. That is nothin' but trouble. Leave it alone. The next thing you know, you got some cat rollin' up on you tryin' to blast you over some pussy, it aint worth it. As a matter of fact, I'll kick your ass myself if you fool with the ho."

"I hear you man, and maybe you're right. That was a nice ass though."

"Yeah, it was nice, but a nice ass can get you killed."

Melvin lifted his glass towards Dave and he in turn lifted his glass of rum and they touched glasses. They continued to drink and talk with the rest of the folks around the bar. It was never mentioned again.

The next morning as he lay there half asleep, a feeling so familiar had begun to pull him from his slumber. He could feel his scrotum being gently fondled, and the heat from warm saliva slide down the shaft of his penis.

He could hear himself moaning just before the cold hit. The stroking and sucking motion went on for several minutes until he came. He slowly opened his eyes, and looked up at the ceiling. "What in the hell are you doin' back here? You've got some nerve, and damn, it's freezin' in here. You'd better get the hell outta here before Dave shows up. What in the hell do you think he'd say? I won't be able to explain this and I really don't feel like hearin' no shit from him today. So you're gonna have to blow this joint right now."

Melvin felt the covers move and her presence pass by him. He pulled the covers high over his head to block the cold. He felt the cold breeze blow through the door and into the hall as the door opened.

Melvin slid the covers down just below his chin and looked over at the nightstand. There he saw the little plastic box.

He rose up from his bed and yelled out, "Marie, you left your damn teeth again! Bring your ass back here and get these damn things. And close that DAMN window before you go! It's freezin'!"

PREVIEW OF THE UPCOMING

NOVEL BY E.L. RHODES

E.L. RHODES

THE SERIALIZATION OF DISCONTENT

A Novel

Chapter 1 - 1957

The sounds of the huge Hammond B3 organ filled the entire room. Mrs. Davis was tickling the black and white keys and mashing the bass pedals on the floor as she rocked in a backward and forward motion. The six-member choir lifted their heads to the heavens as they sang out.

"We've come this faaaaar by faith.........leaning on the Loooooooord."

Willam sat quietly on his mother's lap as she bounced him to the beat of the music. This was their weekly ritual. His mother, Martha Trent, would get up every Sunday morning at 7 a.m. She'd take her shower, get dressed, have her breakfast and then do the same for Willam. Willam Trent was her son, her heart, and her joy.

Actually born William Xavier Trent Jr., he was unfortunately stuck with the first name Willam due to a typographical error on his birth certificate, which his parents never could afford to have corrected. He was small for his age, with caramel colored skin, dark hair, and big brown eyes. He and his mother attended the First Rock Baptist Church of Greater South East. It was a small church, located inside a duplex style house on Chaplin Street in South East Washington D.C. The church only consisted of about forty members, but it had spirit. Willam and his mom Martha never missed a Sunday ever since he was placed on this earth seven months ago. They would attend the eleven o'clock service each Sunday without fail.

Although he was too young to really understand what was going on, he'd sit smiling quietly in his mother's lap, while his mom clapped his hands together during the choir selections. He would stare into the eyes of the pastor during his sermon as if he understood every word.

It was the spring of 1957, a year of segregation, a year of people of color who still struggled endlessly, just to be counted as a people. It was a time when everyone had to do whatever he or she could, just to keep their head above water. But not Willam, he had no worries. He had no fears. He was only seven months old and knew nothing about these things.

This Sunday morning was different than any other Sunday for Willam. This was his first Easter Sunday. The trees and flowers were in bloom and everyone entering the church that day was dapper in their sharp, bright and colorful outfits. Women displayed some of the most stylish hats with brilliant colors, while the men would stride closely behind in their fresh crisp suits. Yes, this was some parade and Willam was enjoying the day.

He sat on his mother's lap as he always did every Sunday. Church went on a little longer than usual. After all, it was Easter.

After the choir had finished singing their last selection and the pastor had ended his sermon, dinners were being served in the kitchen of the church house. Some of the church folk would get a plate to take home because of the limited space. Others would sit and eat wherever there was room.

They would sit on the radiators, the steps, and stools. Folding metal chairs were placed throughout the yard, and were quickly occupied. It looked like a family reunion. This was always one of the biggest events of the year and would go on until late evening every year.

Martha gathered Willam up and retrieved a plate from the kitchen. She took Willam out into the front yard. There were no seats available for Martha, but of course one of the young men was eager to give up his. Remember, this is 1957. Martha spread her wide yellow and white cotton dress across the chair. She sat down slowly not to spill the contents of the plate. She positioned little Willam on her knee, resting his back against her left arm and began eating.

"Would you like a plate for Jimmy, Martha?" Mrs. Gill asked.

Jimmy was Willam's daddy. He was a happy kind of guy who was always laughing, cracking jokes, and dancing, but had the nastiest mean streak, if you took him there. Outside of that, he was a very likable guy and Martha loved him. He was a short man, with dark curly hair and dark skin. He also worked a lot, especially on Sundays and Martha hated that. She'd always tell him, "Sunday is a day for the Lord Jimmy. Keep the Sabbath holy! You need forgiveness Honey, we all do."

Jimmy would always laugh and joke about it. He would start shaking uncontrollably and roll his eyes around in his head yelling, "I got the spirit! I GOT THE SPIRIT! I'm filled with the Holy Ghost! Yeeeeeeeah!"

Then he'd stop and look at her smiling. Of course, she saw NO humor in this. She would scold him a little more and storm off into the kitchen. He'd always finish up with something like, "You wanna be holy? Oh yeah you'll be holy alright, holy shoes, holy blouse, holy everything if I don't make that extra money on Sundays! Just pray for yourself Martha. Don't you worry about me. Lease I aint like those old hypocrites sittin over there hoopin' and hollerin'."

You see, Jimmy, like most other men in the neighborhood, had to work more than one job and Jimmy had more than two. Monday through Friday, he worked as a laborer for a local construction company in the mornings and as a janitor at the D.C. General Hospital in the evenings.

On Sundays he did what most of the other guys did. He hustled.

He would make the weekly liquor run down to Calvert County. He and his good buddy Pete would drive down to

Calvert in a truck owned by Ira. Ira owned the corner grocery store "The Food Plaza", and Pete worked there making deliveries. Pete would sneak the keys every Sunday before they closed, use the truck Sunday night and return the keys bright and early on Monday morning while Ira got the cash registers ready for business. Ira was a Jew, and trusted no one with his money.

They would drive down and meet Hinkly. Hinkly was the biggest white man that Jimmy had ever seen. He and Pete used to joke with him all the time about him being so huge. Hinkly would help them load the liquor into the truck; they'd pay him and he would leave them always with the same warning.

"You boys be careful round these parts. You git caught, you tell on me, you be dead."

He'd smile after saying this, but they both knew that he wasn't kidding.

After finishing her Easter church dinner, Martha made her rounds of hugging and shaking hands with the other members. She had been there for hours. She pulled out the chicken bone that was wedge tightly in Willam's little hand and dropped it into the metal trashcan then headed home.

Martha opened the front door to her home, which was just around the corner from the church. She switched on the fan immediately after stepping inside. She laid out a blanket on the floor in the living room for Willam to rest on, then picked up Jimmy's plate, took it to the kitchen and placed it into the oven. After fixing a cold drink for herself and a bottle for Willam, she bounced back into the living room where they both consumed their beverages. Shortly after, Martha took Willam upstairs, bathed him and got him ready for the night. They went back downstairs and she turned on the television. They were proud of their television. It was black and white of course, but a TV never the less.

"Plop! Plop! Fizz! Fizz! Oh what a relief it is…" they sang on the television advertisement.

Martha adjusted the coat hanger that was used as a television antenna in hopes of clearing up the fuzziness. After some minor adjustments, the picture became clear.

"Gunsmoke? I don't think so young man."

She picked up the pair of pliers lying next to the television, pushed them into the socket and turned the channel.

"Lassie, now that's better. You want to watch Lassie Lil Will?"

After fifteen minutes of Lassie, Willam was fast asleep.

As Willam lay there sleeping, a knock came from the door. It was Mr. Daniels from the church.

Martha placed her index finger to her lips, "Shhhhhhh" then pointed to Willam.

She opened the door. Before stepping in, Mr. Daniels looked in both directions to see if anyone was watching. He entered the living room and sat down on the couch. Martha tiptoed into the kitchen to get him a cold drink. She returned with a glass of rum and ice and sat it on the table in front of Mr. Daniels.

Mr. Daniels was a very tall and very well dressed man who always wore sunglasses. Day or night, he could be seen driving through the neighborhood with those dark plastic eye covers on. He was one of only a few men in the neighborhood who drove a Cadillac and he loved that car. He had it washed daily while he sat in the barber shop chatting and ad drinking. He had a long deep scar on the left side of his face from being cut with a straight razor, but that's the kind of thing you run into when you run numbers.

"Is it cool? I mean, you've got little man right here, and where's Jimmy?"

"It's okay, he's working and my baby's fast asleep. I can take care of you."

Martha leaned over and helped him with his jacket, then his tie. She stood up over him and slipped off her dress. She pulled the white cotton sheet from behind the couch and laid it flat across the plastic covered seat cushions. They then stretched over the sheet covered couch and he took her.

Most men wanted Martha. She was tall and lean, with just enough meat on her to show her curves. She had light brown eyes, and long black wavy hair. Men loved her and she knew how to make them feel good, especially Mr. Daniels. Martha spoke to him the entire time that she was with him. She knew that's what he liked. She knew how arrogant he was and how he liked his ego stroked.

"That's right baby, stroke it just like that! Oh yeah, yeah that's it!"

With her voice climbing higher, Willam was starting to squirm. Martha placed her hands on both sides of Mr. Daniels hips to prevent him from moving.

"Wait!" she whispered.

She pushed him upward and he climbed off.

"Take his little ass upstairs why don't you?"

Martha walked over and patted Willam gently on his back until he squirmed no more.

She walked back over to Mr. Daniels and mounted him. With her hips thrusting as hard as she could, she leaned over and whispered in his ear.

"Give it to me Daddy, give me all you got. Oh, it's sooooo good! Oh yeah baby!"

She continued stroking him until he exploded deep into her. He then tried to kiss Martha, but she pulled back. Her kissing was only for Jimmy.

She immediately climbed off of him, reached over and passed him a few napkins, which were lying on the table behind her. She tipped upstairs to the bathroom, where she cleaned herself quickly before returning to Willam.

"I left the money on the table, Hon. Thanks again."

That's right, this was a regular occurrence, and Mr. Daniel's was a repeat customer. He placed his hat on his head and opened the door then peeked out the screen door, slipped on his shades and made his exit.

Martha had two more similar visits that evening before Jimmy's scheduled arrival.

She made a total of thirty dollars that day.

Jimmy usually would get home about 11 p.m. He had the same routine every night. He would come in the door, kiss Martha, walk upstairs and whisper to Willam as he slept. After about ten minutes, he would make his way back downstairs, grab his plate out of the oven and sit with Martha and watch the "Honeymooners".

After putting little Willam down for his slumber, Martha cleaned the kitchen and did some ironing. She folded all of her laundry and put it neatly in its proper place. She then went downstairs and positioned herself on the couch in preparation for Jimmy's entrance. She watched midget wrestling and "The Jack Benny Show". She liked the character named "Rochester".

She sat there for over an hour watching the screen until she dozed off.

Hours had passed.

The loud constant beep woke Martha from her sleep. It was the sound that followed the playing of the "Star Spangled Banner" every night at the end of the TV station's broadcast. Martha sat there glaring at the large circular black and white object on the television screen. She collected herself and looked over for Jimmy. She walked upstairs and looked in their bedroom but did not see him. After searching every room upstairs, she decided to check in front of the house for his car. Jimmy's car was not there either.

"Where is he?" she thought. "He's probably broken down on 295 again."

She made her way upstairs, not worried and climbed into bed. She never gave it a second thought because it had happened many times before. Jimmy would constantly breakdown, but would not give up that old 1952 Chevy II. It was red and shaped just like a little box. He loved that car.

The next morning Martha was awakened by loud banging on the door. She pulled the sheet back and slid into her slippers.

"Coming, I'll be right there," she yelled down the stairs.

As she approached the door, the loud knocking started again. She gathered her bathrobe then opened the door. On the porch stood two, D.C. metropolitan policemen.

"Mrs. Trent?"

"Yes, I'm Mrs. Trent. What's wrong?"

The blank look on their faces told her that something was wrong, very wrong. She realized that Jimmy had not come home last night.

"My husband, is it my husband? Where is he?"

Willam was beginning to cry. He was awake. Martha stepped away from the door and the officers stepped in. She sat on the couch. Now knowing that he was injured, probably laying in some hospital, all kinds of thoughts were racing through her mind.

"Where is he?!" she yelled out.

The white officer stepped back towards the door and the black officer stepped towards her.

"Mrs. Trent, I'm sorry to inform you that your husband James was killed last night out in Calvert County."

Martha stared at the wall. Willam was crying louder, but she could not hear him. She had blocked him out completely. She fell to her knees and screamed.

"NO LORD! PLEASE NO, NOT HIM!"

She continued to scream and weep. Mrs. Delaney from next door climbed over the rail, which divided the two small houses and rushed in to help. After the policemen left, like a zombie, Martha dragged herself upstairs and fell across her bed. She wept for hours.

After that dreadful day, there was a short investigation into his death. Of course, the murders were never solved - Jimmy's or Pete's. Rumor has it, that night Jimmy and Pete made their regular run down to Calvert County. Hinkly was there to meet them. He helped them load the truck as usual and left. The truck was later found ten miles from their pickup spot, empty. Jimmy was found, just walking distance from the truck. His face had been severely beaten and both of his hands were broken.

The rope had snapped his neck and he swung from that rope all night. His left foot appeared to have been completely blown off by a shotgun blast. As for Pete, he was never found. Jimmy's casket was never opened at his funeral.

READER'S NOTES

www.ingramcontent.com/pod-product-compliance
Lightning Source LLC
Chambersburg PA
CBHW020803250626
47155CB00003B/1186